D0429517

KAT GREENE
COMES CLEAN

KAT GREENE COMES CLEAN

Melissa Roske

WITHDRAWN

🌉 Charlesbridge

To Henry and Chloe: We did it!

Text copyright © 2017 by Melissa Roske
Illustrations copyright © 2017 by Nathan Durfee
All rights reserved, including the right of reproduction in whole or in part in any form.
Charlesbridge and colophon are registered trademarks of Charlesbridge Publishing, Inc.

Published by Charlesbridge, 85 Main Street, Watertown, MA 02472
(617) 926-0329 • www.charlesbridge.com

Library of Congress Cataloging-in-Publication Data
Names: Roske, Melissa, author.
Title: Kat Greene comes clean / Melissa Roske.
Description: Watertown, MA: Charlesbridge, [2017] | Summary: Fifth-grader
Kat Greene is struggling with her boy-crazy best friend, a disappointing role in the
production of *Harriet the Spy* at her progressive New York City school,
and her mother's preoccupation with cleanliness—a symptom of her
worsening obsessive-compulsive disorder.
Identifiers: LCCN 2016024029 (print) | LCCN 2016026591 (ebook) |
ISBN 9781580897761 (reinforced for library use) |
ISBN 9781607349716 (ebook)
Subjects: LCSH: Obsessive-compulsive disorder—Juvenile fiction. | Mothers and
daughters—Juvenile fiction. | Children of divorced parents—Juvenile fiction. |
Alternative schools—Juvenile fiction. | Friendship—Juvenile fiction. | CYAC:
Obsessive-compulsive disorder—Fiction. | Mothers and daughters—
Fiction. | Divorce—Fiction. | Alternative schools—Fiction. | Schools—
Fiction. | Friendship—Fiction.
Classification: LCC PZ7.1.R6737 Kat 2017 (print) | LCC PZ7.1.R6737 (ebook) |
DDC 813.6 [Fic] —dc23
LC record available at https://lccn.loc.gov/2016024029

Printed in the Unitd States of America
(hc) 10 9 8 7 6 5 4 3 2 1

Handlettering by Nathan Durfee
Display type set in Blue Century by T-26
Text type set in Adobe Jenson
Printed by Berryville Graphics in Berryville, Virginia, USA
Color separations by Coral Graphics Services, Inc. in Hicksville, New York, USA
Production supervision by Brian G. Walker
Designed by Susan Mallory Sherman

1.

Ruined

Sometimes it's the little things that get to me. Like an electric toothbrush. Mom's got one in her hand—but it's not for her teeth. She's using it on the kitchen floor. As if this is normal. As if this makes *sense*. I want to sneak back to my room and start the day over, but I can't. Mom's already spotted me. "Look, Kit-Kat," she says, holding up the toothbrush. "The bristles are perfect for cleaning in between the floor tiles. I got the tip from *Good Housekeeping*. Cool, huh?"

That's not the word I'd use.

I grab a blueberry muffin and plunk down at the breakfast bar.

"Wait!" Mom springs up like a jack-in-the-box. "Let me get you a plate."

"That's okay," I say, hopping off my stool. "I'll get it."

"Don't worry," she says. "Just sit."

I could argue, but what's the point? The less I touch, the less Mom has to frantically clean up after me. I go back to my spot at the breakfast bar.

I watch as Mom yanks off her rubber gloves, places them on the counter, and goes over to the sink. She starts washing her hands, scrubbing each finger and around both thumbs, careful not to miss a spot. "I thought you were getting me a plate," I remind her.

"I am," Mom says, reaching for more soap. "Give me a minute."

A *minute?* When Mom washes her hands, it could take all day. This is her new routine. She says it "calms" her, but I'm not so sure. She doesn't look calm to me.

I pick a stray berry from my muffin and pop it in my mouth. "I did really well on my French quiz," I say, hoping Mom will get the hint and stop washing. "Better than Sam Teitelbaum, even. Want to see it?"

Mom dries her hands on a clean dish towel and reaches into the cabinet for a plate. "I'll look at it later, Kit-Kat," she says, "after you leave for school. I promise."

This is a promise Mom won't keep. She'll be cleaning every inch of our apartment—and washing her hands, over and over again—as soon as I'm gone. I finish my muffin and go to my room to get dressed.

When I'm satisfied with my outfit, I grab my jacket from the hall closet, pick up my backpack, and yell good-bye to Mom. Then I go for my sneakers. They're where I left them yesterday: outside the front door, next to the welcome mat. (Shoes aren't allowed inside the apartment.) But something is different about them. It's the shoelaces. Mom has swapped my neon-pink laces for boring old white ones. I pick up my sneakers and stomp back inside.

Mom is back at the sink, polishing the faucet with Dad's old Foo Fighters T-shirt. It was his favorite, with a giant hole under the armpit. I hold up my sneakers. "What did you do with my neon laces? They're gone!"

Mom turns around. "They were grubby, honey. They needed to be replaced."

"No, they didn't. I bought them last week with Halle. She got matching ones. Remember?"

"Of course I remember," Mom says, tugging at the red bandanna covering her honey-blond hair. "But that doesn't change the fact that your laces were dirty. Now, take those sneakers outside. You'll be late for school."

I ignore her. "Where are my shoelaces?"

Mom goes back to polishing the faucet.

"Mom!"

"Okay, okay . . ."

She puts down Dad's T-shirt and peels off her rubber gloves. I watch as she reaches into a drawer underneath the counter and roots around for my laces. When she puts them in my hand, my heart does an elevator drop. My neon-pink laces are now the soft pink color of a girl's baby blanket. "What did you do?" I say, staring at the faded laces. "Bleach them?"

Mom bites her lip. "I'm sorry, Kit-Kat. I wasn't thinking."

"But you ruined them!"

"I'll buy you new ones."

"That's not the point."

Mom throws up her hands. "I said I was sorry, and I mean it. What else do you want me to do?"

I know *exactly* what Mom can do. I race to my room, snatch my French quiz off my desk, and sprint back to the kitchen. I hold the quiz under Mom's nose. "You said you'd look at this. Now look!"

Mom's eyes dart back to the sink.

Without warning, hot, angry tears spring to my eyes, but I quickly squeeze them away. I won't let Mom get to me. Not this time. I hold the quiz high over my head and let go, watching the paper spiral through the air and land at Mom's bare feet.

She looks more surprised than mad. "What was that for?"

For caring more about a clean kitchen than my French quiz!

For ruining my new shoelaces with bleach.

For scrubbing the floor with an electric toothbrush.

But I don't say any of this. Instead, I bend down to pick up my quiz, crumple it in a tight little ball, and toss it in the trash. I leave for school without saying good-bye.

In the elevator I take out my phone to text Halle. She'll be expecting me on the corner of Thirteenth Street and Seventh Avenue for our daily walk to school. But after my fight with Mom, I'm in no mood for company. I text her.

Don't wait. I went in early. See u at school!

My words are cheerier than I feel.

2.

The Harriet Project

I probably set the record for fastest walk to school ever. (It's only three blocks, but still.) I'm already at my desk when Halle walks in. "Did you notice Michael McGraw's high-tops?" she asks, nodding at her crush across the room. "They're new, in case you were wondering."

I wasn't.

Halle takes out her binders and plops down next to me. "He had them on yesterday until PE. Then he changed into his Vans. He must've gotten a blister." She leans across my desk until her face is within inches of mine. So close, I can smell the onion bagel on her breath. "I wonder where he bought them," Halle continues. "Village Shoes, on Bleecker? Or maybe that sneaker store by the subway. You know the one I'm talking about . . . David Z.?"

Before Halle has time to start naming every shoe store in our Greenwich Village neighborhood—or in all of Manhattan—our teacher, Jane, waves her arms for attention. When no one looks up, she marches over to the metal gong on her desk and whacks it with a mallet. This seems to do the trick, because everyone, including Kevin Cusak, who's been parading around the room with a Burger King crown on his head, shuts up immediately. "I have an important announcement to make," Jane says, putting down the mallet. "Who wants to hear it?"

"Not me!" Kevin yells, adjusting his crown.

Based on all the movies I've seen and books I've read, in most schools disrespectful kids get sent to the principal. But Village Humanity is not like most schools. Halle and I call it Village Calamity because sometimes this place feels like a disaster zone. We don't get report cards, our lockers are padlock-free, and we have one teacher, Jane, for most academic subjects. On days like this, when I'm feeling crabby and nothing's going right, I wish I could go to a more normal school. A place where kids know better than to talk back to their teachers and march around with Burger King crowns on their heads. But that's not going to happen. My mom is a proud graduate of the class of 1989 and I'm keeping the tradition "alive." (Her words.)

"As I was saying," Jane continues, "next week we will start working on the Harriet project, ending with the dramatic presentation of Louise Fitzhugh's 1964 classic, *Harriet the Spy*. In cooperative pairs you will analyze key characters from the book—Harriet and her friend Sport, for instance—and present your characters, in full costume, at the Thanksgiving assembly. I've taken the liberty of assigning partners."

Halle and I turn to each other in alarm. Having to present in front of the whole school is bad enough, but with assigned partners too? Normally we choose our own. Still, the project could be fun, as long as I'm Harriet. I've read the book before and know that we are a lot alike. For one thing, Harriet is an only child like me (well, the way I used to be, before Dad married Barbara and my little brother, Henry, came along). For another, we both live in New York City. We both have long straight hair (I wear mine in pigtails), and we both love cake. Oh, and we each have a parent who loves math. (That'd be my dad.) *Yuck.*

"I call Sport!" Kevin yells from the back of the room.

"No, *I'm* Sport!" Michael yells over him. "I play baseball."

"So what?" Kevin says. "I play baseball. And basketball, and hockey, and soccer, and—"

"Being good at sports has nothing to do with it," Sam Teitelbaum tells the boys, fiddling with his asthma inhaler. "It's charisma that counts."

"I've got charisma," Michael says.

Madeline Langford rolls her eyes. "You don't even know what it *means*. Or how to spell it."

"He does too," Halle says, jumping to her crush's defense. "Tell her, Michael."

"Well . . ."

"People!" It's Jane, at the end of her rope. "Please."

I listen for my name as Jane starts reading off her list. "Kevin and Madeline, you will be Marion Hawthorne and Rachel Hennessey." I smile, relieved I wasn't chosen as one of the mean girls. I'm not sure I could pull it off.

Kevin is out of his seat like a rocket. "I'm not playing a girl. No *way*."

Jane purses her lips. "You know we're flexible about gender roles at this school, Kevin. We don't make assumptions about how a person should look or act based on gender—or on religion, ethnicity, or race, for that matter. It's not the Village Humanity way. Now, please sit down."

When I look over at Halle, her hand is in the air. "Are there any black kids in the book?" she asks Jane.

I think I know why Halle's asking. Her dad is white and her mom is black. She makes jokes sometimes about the weird stares her family gets from people on the street, but I know she doesn't really think it's funny.

"Halle raises an important point," Jane tells the class. "But to your question, Halle, I'm afraid the answer is no—not in this particular book. Though I assure you there will be others this year that do include persons of color."

"What about people who speak Spanish?" Hector Rodriguez asks.

Jane shakes her head. "*Harriet the Spy* was written more than fifty years ago, and in some ways it can feel dated, especially if we compare Harriet's classroom to ours. That said, I strongly believe that every book we'll read in fifth grade—including those with characters who look different from us—contains something of value for *everyone*. Does that make sense?"

"Maybe . . ." Halle says.

She seems doubtful, but I already know a million ways Harriet, Halle, and I are alike. I make a mental note to share this with Halle at lunch.

Jane goes back to her clipboard. "Hector and Liberty . . . Mr. and Mrs. Welsch—"

Kevin's hand flies up.

"What is it *now*, Kevin?" Jane looks ready to stick him in the supply closet.

"How come Hector gets to play a guy? No fair!"

Jane lets out the biggest sigh ever. "If you've been listening to the discussion—which I suspect you haven't—it's your assumption that's unfair. It's equally possible Hector will be *Mrs.* Welsch."

Now Hector is on his feet, his belly jiggling under his T-shirt. "I'm *Mr.* Welsch!"

While Jane referees the boys' argument, I pray for a decent partner. Halle is my first choice (obviously), but Jane would never put us together. We'd have too much fun. That leaves Michael and Sam. Then I hear my name.

I will be working with Sam, and our assigned characters are Pinky Whitehead (Sam) and The Boy with the Purple Socks (me). This means: (a) I don't get to be Harriet and (b) I'm stuck with the most boring character in the book. As Harriet says, The Boy with the Purple Socks is so boring, no one bothers to remember his real name. *Great.*

Sam is more enthusiastic than I am. "Awesome!" He leans over to give me a high five. "We should get started right away, Kat. Like today, after school. I have the allergist at four, but I could come over after that."

"No, that's okay," I say, knowing Mom's behavior lately is too weird for random guests. "We have plenty of time. The Thanksgiving assembly isn't until the end of November. That's more than two months away."

"True," Sam says, pushing up his glasses. "But excellence can't be rushed. We need to formulate our strategy now to get ahead of the competition."

"The competition?" I try not to laugh. Kevin's got two pencils up his nose, pretending to be a walrus; Wilson Cheung-Levy is taking Liberty Alfredo's temperature with a digital thermometer; and Hector has written HELP ME on his belly in Sharpie. I point this out to Sam.

"Well, yeah," he says, "but—"

"Oh, my God. Oh, my God. Oh, my *God* . . ." It's Halle, muttering under her breath.

"What's up with her?" Sam wants to know.

I was wondering the same thing. I lean over and grab my best friend's arm. "What's going on, Hal? Are you okay?"

Halle mashes her lips together and shakes her head from side to side.

"Maybe she needs to go to the nurse," Sam says. "She doesn't look too good."

Sam is right. Halle's eyes are glassy as marbles. They're also laser-focused on something across the room. I follow her gaze until I see why she's lost the ability to speak.

Of course.

Halle's been partnered with Michael. I must have missed the announcement while Sam was talking about meeting up after school.

"I can't believe I'm Harriet's *nanny*," Michael says, coming over to our table. "That totally sucks."

"Oh, it *does*, Michael." Halle is leaning so far forward in her chair, I'm worried she might fall off. "I know how badly you wanted Sport. It's so unfair."

"Ole Golly's not that bad," I say, remembering how cool she is, and how much Harriet loves her. "She's the most important person in Harriet's life. More important than her parents, even."

Michael turns to me with a smile. "I never thought of it that way, Kat. Thanks! Who's your character?"

"The Boy with the Purple Socks," I say, wrinkling up my nose. "BO-*ring*."

"Maybe he's cooler than you think," Michael says. "Just like Ole Golly." He smiles at me again before returning to his seat.

When he's gone, Halle flops back like a rag doll. "This project is going to be better than I thought," she says, offering me and Sam a lopsided grin. "Like, *a lot* better."

Maybe for her, I think—and for Sam. But for me? Not so much.

3.

Humans Versus Bananas

"I can't believe Michael is my Harriet partner," Halle says as we leave school later that afternoon. "I'm so lucky." She hooks her arm through mine as we round Tenth Street and head down Seventh Avenue for home.

I should be happy for her, but how can I? Halle gets to play Harriet and I don't. And the worst part? She doesn't even care. All that matters to her is that she can hang out with Michael and call it "homework." I would've given anything to play Harriet. Life is so unfair.

Halfway down the block, Halle squats down next to a hydrant to pick up a Snapple cap. "You know what Michael did when he found out we were partners?" she says, handing it to me. "He *smiled*."

"That's nice," I say, taking the cap. It's for my collection. I have at least fifty, stashed in an old coffee can at the back of my closet. Mom would freak if she knew I collected caps from my friends and the recycling bins at school—let alone off the sidewalk. As she says, New York City is a breeding ground for germs.

I turn the cap over and read the Real Fact out loud: "Humans share fifty percent of their DNA with bananas."

"That's ridiculous," Halle says, getting to her feet. "Totally untrue."

"How do you know?" I say. "You're not exactly a scientist."

"Duh. All I'm saying is, it's highly doubtful that a human being has *that* much in common with a piece of fruit!"

Sometimes my best friend can be more stubborn than my three-year-old brother. "Sorry. I just meant the banana thing must be true. Otherwise, the Snapple people wouldn't put it on a cap. It would make them look stupid. These caps don't lie."

"I guess." Halle helps me scope the sidewalk for more caps. Suddenly she stops short, narrowly missing a little kid whizzing by on a red scooter. "Do you think Michael likes me?" she asks. "Be honest."

Oh no. I'd rather go back to talking about bananas. But Halle doesn't want to talk about bananas. She wants me to tell her that Michael likes her. But how can

I do that? From what I've heard, he prefers Madeline Langford, who has real diamond earrings and something to put in her bra.

I decide to play it cool. "Maybe he does like you," I say, kicking at a blob of bubble gum squished into the sidewalk. "Anything's possible."

Halle crosses her arms over her chest. "Thanks a lot, Kat!"

I should've known Halle would take my comment the wrong way. I start again. "What I meant was, it's *possible* Michael likes you, but how would I know? We're not exactly BFFs."

Halle uncrosses her arms. "Good point."

I'm in no big rush to get home, but I motion for Halle to hurry up. All this talk about her crush is getting on my nerves. "You won't believe what my mom did this morning," I say, changing the subject.

Halle scratches her head. "Used a new feather duster on the lampshades?"

"Nope."

"Combed the fringe on the Persian rug?"

"Guess again."

"Bleached your underwear?"

"Close."

When I tell her about the electric toothbrush, the laces, and the hand-washing, Halle's eyes go wide as saucers. "Are you going to tell your dad?"

I shake my head. "If he knew how bad Mom's cleaning

has gotten lately, he'd make me live uptown with him and Barbara and Henry."

"That would stink," Halle says.

"Yeah," I say, nodding. "It kind of would." I love my dad—don't get me wrong. I like my stepmom too. Even my little brother is bearable when he's not throwing a tantrum or whining for gummy worms. But home is where Mom is, even if she ruins my shoelaces and cleans the floor with an electric toothbrush. I just wish home didn't feel so weird these days.

Halle and I continue down Seventh Avenue in silence. When we reach Thirteenth Street, Halle squints up at me, shading her eyes from the hazy September sun. "Kat?"

"Yeah?"

"Did you notice how good Michael's hair looked in PE? I think he's using gel. Or maybe he's just styling it differently. What do you think?"

I think that if Halle keeps this up, I may need to start wearing earplugs. But that's not what I say. Instead, I promise to check out Michael's hair tomorrow and that I'll text her later, when I'm done with my homework. If Harriet's taught me one thing, it's that you don't want those closest to you to know *everything* you're thinking. It will only land you in trouble.

4.

An Inconvenient Coincidence

I'm surprised to find Mom locking the front door when I get off the elevator. "Where are we going?" I ask, eyeing her outfit. "You're still in your cleaning clothes."

Mom looks down at her faded overalls and touches the red bandanna covering her hair. "That's okay. We're just going to the supermarket."

"We are?"

Mom nods. "I want to get steaks for dinner."

"Do I have to go too?"

"You know I'm not thrilled about leaving you alone in the apartment," Mom says. "Don't give me a hard time, Kat."

Me give *her* a hard time? That's a good one. Mom should've gotten the steaks while I was at school. And she shouldn't have ruined my shoelaces or made me so angry that I trashed my French quiz. Dad would have been so proud of it. "Can I put this inside first?" I ask, turning around to show Mom my backpack. "It's heavy."

Mom looks at me as if I've asked to dunk my head in a public toilet. "Before you've wiped it down? That backpack contains more germs than the bottom of your shoe!" She reaches into the pocket of her overalls and pulls out a packet of antibacterial wipes. "Here," she says, thrusting the packet at me. "I'll wait."

Mom's carrying wipes in her pocket now? *Seriously?* I know she has a thing about germs and is worried I might get sick (at least that's what she's been telling me lately), but this is too much. "It's okay," I tell her, hoisting my backpack higher on my shoulder. "I'll leave my bag downstairs." Mom shrugs and follows me down the hall.

"How was school?" she asks in the elevator. She digs through her purse and produces a tiny bottle of Purell. I watch as she squirts the clear, oozy liquid onto her hands and rubs them together. Her fingers are as red as lobster claws. Cracked and scaly too.

"It was fine," I say, accepting the bottle she's handing me, "but you'll never guess who I got for the Harriet project. It's so unfair, but—"

Mom grabs my arm. "I forgot something."

"Mom . . ."

"No, I'd better go back upstairs. Wait for me in the lobby, Kat."

"You're going to wash your hands again, aren't you?"

"I'm sorry," she says softly. The look she gives me is so sad, it's impossible to stay mad at her. I just wish I understood what was going on.

I get off the elevator and bring my backpack into the package room for safekeeping. Then I flop into the armchair opposite the front desk and wait. Ten minutes later, Mom is back without an apology or an excuse. We both know what took her so long, but neither of us says anything. What is there to say, really? I zip up my jacket and follow Mom out of the building.

My neighborhood buzzes with the sounds of taxi horns. Bikes whizz down Seventh Avenue and people hustle along the sidewalks, walking dogs and pushing strollers. I see a little kid hopping off the school bus, struggling under the weight of his too-heavy backpack. He smiles when he sees his mom, or maybe it's his nanny. I used to have a nanny when I was little—Sonia, who made Jamaican beef patties and sang "Hush, Baby, Hush" at naptime. I loved her the way Harriet loves Ole Golly. Sonia left when Mom lost her magazine job and decided to stay home with me. I'd hoped Mom would learn to make beef patties and sing "Hush, Baby, Hush" like Sonia, but she didn't. She subscribed to *Good Housekeeping* and bought a new mop.

Mom steers me across the street and into the super-market. A blast of arctic air greets me as we enter through the automatic doors. I'm wishing I'd worn a heavier jacket when Mom pulls out two pairs of latex gloves. She hands one pair to me.

"Tell me you're kidding," I say. "Please."

"If you knew how much bacteria are on the handle of a shopping cart, you wouldn't argue," she says. "Now, put on the gloves." Mom gives her own gloves a quick tug and stretches them over her hands.

"Can't I use hand sanitizer?" I ask, pointing to the Purell station next to the entrance. "Or just not touch anything?"

Mom's lips disappear in a thin, angry line. "Come on, Kat. Don't be difficult."

She wants me to wear latex gloves in public, and *I'm* the difficult one? Please. I take the gloves and follow my mom down the produce aisle, where she stops in front of a display of cantaloupes. She picks one up and sniffs it. Then she gives it a sharp thump to see if it's ripe and puts it in the shopping cart.

"I thought we were just getting steaks," I say.

"I did say that," Mom admits. "But now that we're here, we may as well pick up a few other things. This won't take a minute."

Now, where have I heard that one before?

I try to keep up as Mom zips through Produce, turns right at Frozen Foods, and stops in Paper and

Cleaning Supplies. While she's filling the cart with enough paper towels to wipe down the Statue of Liberty, something bright and glittery catches my eye. It's a diamond, which is attached to an ear, which is attached to a girl. A girl who has something to put in her bra and thinks Halle's crush has no charisma.

Crud! What is Madeline doing here?

"Deidre?" It's Madeline's mother calling over from Canned Goods. "Great to see you! It's been, like, forever."

"You too, Stacey." Mom pushes her cart closer to Mrs. Langford. "It has been a while."

"We missed having you on the benefit committee last spring," Madeline's mom says, balancing her grocery basket against her hip. "We really could have used your help."

"Well . . ." Mom tugs at her bandanna.

While Mom and Mrs. Langford continue their conversation by the cranberry sauce, I notice Madeline scratching a mosquito bite on her left knee. She scowls when she catches me looking. "What are you staring at?" she asks.

"Nothing," I say.

Madeline points to my hands. "What's with the rubber gloves?"

I stuff my hands in my pockets. "None of your business."

"Freak."

As I'm praying for the moms to wrap it up, I catch my mom reaching into her pocket for the antibacterial wipes. She wipes down a can of diced pineapple, places it in her cart, and reaches for another can.

"What is your mom doing?" Madeline wants to know.

"Well . . ." I rack my brain for a good excuse. "She read an article about an E. coli outbreak at a supermarket in Yorkville—right around the corner from my dad's, actually—and she wants to be on the safe side. You can never be too careful, right?"

The corners of Madeline's mouth creep up in a smirk. "Maybe," she says, "but I don't think you can catch E. coli from a can of pineapple."

"How do you know?"

"I don't. But using antibacterial wipes in public is crazy, E. coli or not."

My hands clench into fists. I'm mad at Mom for embarrassing me, but I'm madder at Madeline for saying my mom is crazy. "Shut up," I say.

"Make me," Madeline says, lifting her chin.

Mrs. Langford comes to the rescue. "Maddy and I need to get a move on," she says, putting a French-manicured hand on her daughter's arm. "See you guys around."

I breathe a sigh of relief. My humiliation is coming to an end.

Or maybe not.

"Chanel!"

Before I can say, "Please kill me now," Madeline's mother is welcoming Chanel Steinberg, Coco's mom, to Canned Goods. Coco is bringing up the rear, her hand deep in a bag of trail mix.

"What a crazy coincidence," Mrs. Langford squeals, kissing Mrs. Steinberg on the cheek. "How *are* you?"

While the mothers continue to talk, Coco walks up to Madeline. "What's going on?"

I hold my breath, waiting for Madeline to make fun of my mom. She's still wiping down cans at the other end of the aisle. Luckily, Mrs. Langford chooses that moment to appear with her basket. "The checkout line is getting longer by the minute," she says to Madeline. "We should go."

"Us too," Mrs. Steinberg says, sidling up to Coco. "Come on, honey."

Madeline's mother turns to me with an awkward smile. "Take care of yourself, Kat." I can tell she feels sorry for me, which makes my face burn. She gives me a little wave and runs off to join the others.

Now it's just me and Mom.

I head down the aisle, where she's still wiping down cans. "Mom," I say, touching her shoulder. "Stop."

"I'm almost done," she says, cleaning a can of peaches in heavy syrup before placing it in her cart. "Give me a minute."

"Mom," I say more urgently. "Please."

She whips her head around. "I said I'm almost done, Kat, and I mean it. Be patient."

"Take all the time you want," I say, heading for the exit. "I'm leaving."

I expect Mom to run after me. To say eleven-year-olds shouldn't cross Fourteenth Street by themselves. It's a wide, busy street, and getting hit by a cab—or worse, the crosstown bus—is a real possibility. But she doesn't. She picks up another can and starts wiping.

5.

Rap Session

On the walk to school the next day, I'm dying to tell Halle what happened at the supermarket, but her mind is elsewhere. "Did you know that Michael is a Scorpio?" she asks, bending down to pick up a fallen leaf. "It's the most misunderstood of all the zodiac signs." She inspects her find and places it in her backpack. "They're also very emotional."

"I didn't know that," I say. "I'm a Leo, but I'm not sure what it means in terms of my personality. I'm supposed to be lucky with money, though." I dig in my pocket and produce a crumpled dollar. "See? I found it yesterday outside my building."

"It's true," Halle says, back on the move and clearly not listening to a word I'm saying. "Look at Michael. He seems cool on the outside, but there's a lot going on under the surface. *Deep* stuff."

I'm not sure how Halle came to this conclusion, but I decide to take her word for it. If she wants to think her crush is deep, that's fine with me. I have other things to worry about—namely Mom.

When she came home from the supermarket last night, she knocked on my door and begged me to open up. She even pushed my crinkled-up French quiz under the door with a yellow sticky note on it.

Nice job, Kit-Kat! I'm so proud of you! Xox, Mom

This was a really big deal, because she dug it out of the trash. But still, I wouldn't let her in. I put in my earbuds and turned up the music. I didn't speak to her at breakfast this morning, and I haven't decided whether I'll talk to her later, when I get home. It all depends on my mood, and how long I can hold a grudge.

At school, Jane is already banging the gong for attention when Halle and I walk in. We quickly take our seats.

"Simmer down, people!" Jane says, waving the mallet over her head. "I need all eyes on me." She waits until the room is quiet before putting down the mallet. "I have a treat for you," she tells us. "Olympia Rabinowitz is coming to our classroom for a rap session. She'll be here any minute."

Halle and I exchange looks. Olympia is the school psychologist, and it's safe to say that a rap session—some kind of hippie-dippie share-a-thon, I'm guessing—doesn't count as a "treat."

Michael puts up his hand. "I have a problem."

"Yes?" Jane crosses her arms over her corduroy jumper.

"I haven't done my Christmas shopping yet."

Jane frowns. "What does Christmas shopping have to do with Olympia's visit to our classroom, Michael? Besides, it's the middle of September."

Michael takes off his Yankees cap and puts it on backward. "You said we were having a wrap session, but I have nothing to *wrap*."

Jane's eyes shoot up to the ceiling. "We're not wrapping presents, Michael. The fifth grade will be having a rap session. Rap, as in R-A-P. You know, a discussion. A chance to share our feelings."

Madeline, who's been checking her hair for split ends, raises her hand. "We won't be talking about anything personal, will we? Like periods? Because if we are, I'm not saying anything with the boys around."

Wilson looks up from the book he's reading, *Human Anatomy and Physiology*. "Menstruation is nothing to be embarrassed about," he says. "It's a perfectly normal bodily function."

"*I'm* not embarrassed," Madeline says huffily, "but some of the boys in this class are too immature to handle it." She turns around to give Kevin a pointed stare.

"Immature?" Kevin lets out a snort. "The men don't care about that stuff anyway."

"Men?" Madeline looks around the room. "I don't see any men."

Jane's had enough. "We will discuss all subjects as they arise. Now, if there are no more questions—"

"Hello, hello . . . ?" It's Olympia Rabinowitz, here for our first rap session. Her hair is the color of orange Kool-Aid and styled in lots of skinny braids. "Thank you for allowing me into your learning space," Olympia says, extending her arms wide. "This will be a groovy experience . . . for all of us."

Groovy? I wait for someone to laugh, but the room is as quiet as a library. Even Kevin has his mouth shut.

Olympia strides to the front of the room and sits down on the edge of Jane's desk. "Sharing our thoughts and feelings in a safe, judgment-free space is vitally important for any group—whether that group is a family at home, or a family in the classroom." She pushes up the sleeves of her oversize ski sweater and beams at the class. "That's why confidentiality is key."

After Sam explains to Michael that confidentiality is a fancy word for "Don't blab other people's secrets," Olympia nods. "That's right, Sam. Whatever you say in this room *stays* in this room."

"Like Vegas!" Hector reaches over to bump fists with Kevin.

"Huh?" Michael doesn't get it.

"It's an expression, butt-brain," Kevin tells him. "Whatever happens in Vegas stays in Vegas."

"*Las* Vegas," Sam corrects him, "in the state of Nevada, the thirty-sixth state admitted to the Union on October 31, 1864."

"My grandma went to Las Vegas once," Michael says, leaning back in his chair. "She won four hundred dollars and a free steak dinner."

"Red meat is disgusting!" Liberty scrunches up her nose.

"And very unhealthy," Wilson adds, tapping his medical book. "It clogs the arteries and causes hypertension."

"I hope your grandma chose the vegetarian option," Liberty says to Michael. "Did she?"

Michael frowns. "I'm not sure. Can I borrow your phone?"

Jane clears her throat. "While the importance of a vegetarian diet can't be underestimated, Olympia is waiting to begin."

Olympia hops off the desk and starts arranging our chairs in a "trust circle." Once we're all seated, she reaches into her *Free Tibet* tote and pulls out a long wooden stick. "This is an aboriginal talking stick," Olympia tells the class, dropping her voice to a hush. "A symbol of tolerance and democracy. Whoever holds the stick has the right to speak. Others may not interrupt without the speaker's permission. Now, who would like to kick things off?"

Michael flings up his arm. "Me!"

Olympia gets up from the trust circle and hands him the stick. "Speak your truth, Michael. Loud and proud."

Michael clears his throat. "Well, there's someone in this room I really like. She's nice, and cool, and funny. But I don't think she likes me. It sucks, you know?"

I hold my breath, waiting for Olympia to get mad at Michael for using the word "sucks." She doesn't. "This must be very hard for you," Olympia says, returning to her seat. "Have you told this girl how you feel?" I like that Olympia asked Michael a question rather than telling him what to do. Grown-ups hardly ever do that.

"No," Michael says, shaking his head. "That would be weird."

Olympia leans forward. "Weird in what way?"

"I dunno. Just weird."

Halle pokes me in the arm. "He's talking about me."

"How do you know?" I whisper.

"Look." Halle makes a pecking motion with her head. I follow her eyeballs and see that she's right: Michael is staring straight at her. And all this time I thought he liked Madeline! Which goes to show: diamond earrings and a bra can only get you so far.

Then again, what if I'm wrong and Michael really does prefer Madeline? Halle will be crushed, like she was in third grade when her mom wouldn't let her get her ears pierced. But this is more serious. This is boy stuff.

"Kat?" It's Olympia, squatting in front of me with the talking stick. "Would you like a turn? I heard you whispering to Halle."

"No, thanks," I say quickly. "I'm fine."

"Are you sure?"

I have to think twice before answering. The truth is, I'm *not* fine. I'm so mad at Mom I could scream. Why is she so focused on cleaning and germs these days? Why did she have to embarrass me at the supermarket in front of Madeline and Coco? And why did she let me walk home by myself? Sure, Greenwich Village is safe, safer than when Mom was a girl and she had to carry mugger money in her Care Bears lunch box. But that doesn't mean I liked walking home by myself. It's only fun when you want to walk home alone. Not when you have to.

"Kat?" Olympia is looking up at me now. Her eyes are the color of faded Levi's, with lashes so pale they're almost white.

"I don't have anything to say," I tell her, shrugging off the talking stick. "Sorry."

Olympia gives me a warm, crinkly-eyed smile. "Maybe next time," she says, getting to her feet.

Yeah, I think. *Next time.*

Or maybe not.

6.

Dirty Laundry

I catch up to Halle in the cafeteria, in line for spaghetti and soy balls. She wants to analyze Michael's rap-session confession, but I stop her before she gets going. I need to tell her about my problems or I'll explode. I get a tray of food and sit down across from her.

"I can't believe Madeline and Coco were there," Halle says after I've filled her in about the supermarket disaster. "I bet you wanted to die."

"Death," I say, reaching for a napkin, "would have been a relief."

"You should tell your dad," Halle says, spearing a soy ball with her fork. "Maybe your mom has some kind of problem. I mean, who brings antibacterial wipes to the supermarket? And wears latex gloves?"

That's what I'd like to know. I watch Halle chew.

Suddenly she puts down her fork. "I have an idea."

"Yeah?"

"You should ask Olympia for advice. Psychologists deal with stuff like this all the time. She'll know exactly what to do!"

"Olympia? You can't be serious?" I get up with my tray.

"Come on, Kat," Halle says, grabbing my sleeve. "Hear me out."

I sit back down. "You've got twenty seconds. Go."

As Halle tries to convince me that Olympia is the answer to my problems, I start to wonder whether my best friend is right. Olympia is a professional psychologist after all, and she does seem nice. She even stopped me in the hall after the rap session to apologize for putting me on the spot. "Come by my office if you ever feel like talking," she said. "My door is always open."

But who am I kidding? It's nice to know Olympia cares, but Mom would kill me if I told a stranger about what's going on. As she likes to say, it's tacky to air your dirty laundry in public. Which means I'm keeping my laundry right where it is: in the hamper, with the lid shut tight.

※

Mom is vacuuming the sofa cushions when I get home from school. I consider saying hello, but I don't have it in me. Instead, I go to my room and flop down with

Harriet the Spy. I'm at the part where Harriet tells her parents she won't go to dancing school, but I can't concentrate. My brain keeps replaying what Halle said to me at lunch.

You should ask Olympia for advice.

Psychologists deal with stuff like this all the time.

She'll know exactly what to do!

What if Halle is right? What if talking to Olympia isn't such a dumb idea after all?

I put down my book and go get my Village Calamity laptop. We all got one this year, with a school email account and everything. I haven't emailed anybody yet, but here it is—all set up for me. I start typing.

TO: Olympia.Rabinowitz@VillageHumanity.org
SUBJECT: Help
DATE: September 15 4:07:42 PM EDT
FROM: Kat.Greene@VillageHumanity.org

Dear Olympia,

Halle told me to write to you. She thinks you might be able to help me with a problem. A problem with my mom.

This may sound weird, but my mom has this thing about cleaning. She does it all the time, for hours and hours, every single day. Weekends too. She's always been a neat freak, even before my parents got divorced four years ago, but lately things seem extra strange. She started washing her hands a lot and spraying Lysol on the doorknobs and light switches. Sometimes she'll do the same load of dishes over and over again, just to make sure they're really clean. She says she can't help it, which I don't understand. I mean, I used to bite my nails and thought I couldn't help it. But last year I decided to stop—so I did. Why can't my mom do the same thing with cleaning?

Oh, and get this: Yesterday, she wore latex gloves at the supermarket and made me wear them too. Then she wiped down cans with antibacterial wipes while people were watching. (By "people," I mean Madeline and Coco, who were there with their moms.) This can't be normal, whether you're a neat freak or not.

Whenever I've asked my mom about all the cleaning she's been doing, she tells me not to worry. But that's easy for her to say. She's not the one who has to sit around while she makes everything clean— and then clean again—before we go anywhere or do anything. And she's not the one who can't have friends over because they'll track in germs. Not that I'd want my friends to come over. They'd think my mom's weird. Except Halle, of course. Best friends don't care if your mom is weird or not.

Today in rap session you asked Michael if he's told the girl he likes how he feels. I bet you'll tell me to tell my mom how I feel. I don't think I could do that, though. That's why I'm writing to you.

-Kat

I read over my email. The words look fine on the computer screen, but there's so much more I could say. For one thing—and maybe most important of all—I want my mom to act normal, the way she did before Dad moved out and started his new family uptown.

My parents used to be happy together, and I have a picture to prove it, in a silver frame on my desk: Mom and Dad at my cousin Katie's bat mitzvah, mugging for the camera. I was only six, but I remember how Dad told the photographer to hang on a sec while he snatched a yellow rose from the flower arrangement and stuck it between his teeth. Mom had rolled her eyes and said, "Really, Dennis?" but I could tell she thought it was funny too. My parents got divorced a year later. Then Dad met Barbara in line at Starbucks, and that was that. Henry was born when I was eight.

I take one last look at my email, then drag it into the trash. There's no way I can send it. What was I thinking, telling Olympia about Mom? I find my phone and call Halle. Sometimes, there's nothing like hearing your best friend's voice when you feel like crud.

"Why'd you trash the email?" Halle asks. "You should've sent it. It was a good idea."

"I don't want Olympia to think my mom is a freak," I say. "Only I can think that."

"Yeah, but Olympia would never think that. She's a psychologist."

"Maybe . . ."

I know Halle is trying to say all the right things. But I still can't picture myself sharing my problems with Olympia—even if I want to.

After I hang up, Mom appears at my door. She's holding a bottle of disinfectant spray and an almost-empty roll of paper towels. "Would you mind running down to the deli for a few things, Kit-Kat? It's still light outside, and dinner won't be ready for at least an hour."

I don't want to run down to the deli, even if it is only around the corner and Omar will give me free pickles and tell me how business is going. Still, I ask Mom what she wants.

"Oh, not much." Mom reaches into the pocket of her overalls and pulls out a list. "Paper towels, a bottle of Windex, two cans of Lysol . . ."

Suddenly that email to Olympia doesn't sound like such a bad idea.

7.

Clean Sweep

Mom is doing something other than cleaning when I get home from the deli. She's sprawled out on the couch, watching TV, a bowl of popcorn in her lap. This is odd. Mom hardly ever watches TV, at least not without a mop or a dust rag in her hand. And popcorn? In Mom's world, those pesky little kernels are a bear to vacuum up. Maybe I don't need to write to Olympia after all. Mom looks happier and more relaxed than I've seen her in a long time.

"What's going on?" I ask, pointing to the screen. "Are you feeling okay?"

Mom laughs. "I'm fine. Come sit." She passes me the popcorn as I sink into the cushions. For a split second,

I'm transported back to when Mom and I had Girls' Nights, when we'd watch movies like *The Parent Trap* and *Freaky Friday* with popcorn and big bowls of ice cream on our laps. Dad joined us sometimes, but not usually. It was always me and Mom.

I'm trying to remember the last Girls' Night we had when Mom grabs my arm. "It's starting!" she says, squealing like a first grader at a birthday party. "Watch."

My eyes settle on a tall, silver-haired man holding a broom. He jogs across the set—a pretend kitchen— and gives a cheesy grin to the camera. When he gets to the other side, he hands his broom to a burly sanitation worker in a green uniform and orange safety vest. The guy takes the broom, holds it up in the air, and gives it a little twirl.

"What *is* this?" I ask.

Mom shushes me.

Oh, *boy*. I sit back and watch a second sanitation worker jog across the TV kitchen and accept a broom from the man with the silver hair. Then another, and another. Before long, five sanitation workers, two men and three women, are standing in a row with their brooms. When the music stops, a huge neon sign lights up behind them: CLEAN SWEEP.

Oh, *now* I get it. The sanitation workers are actually contestants on a game show!

"Isn't this great?" Mom says, her eyes twinkling like Christmas lights.

"I guess. . . ."

"Each contestant is given four dirty household items to clean," Mom tells me, using the remote as a pointer. "A greasy stove, a refrigerator with moldy food inside, an old barbecue grill, and a toilet. They get to choose their own cleaning supplies too. Whoever cleans their items the fastest and most effectively wins."

"Wins the stuff?"

"Nope, even better. Twenty-five thousand dollars in cash and a lifetime supply of cleaning products."

"Really?"

"Really. I'd be perfect for this, and I wouldn't have to travel. The show is taped right here in New York." Mom gestures to the TV. "I'm going to fill out an application," she says. "What do you think?"

I want to say that cleaning a dirty toilet on national TV is the silliest thing I've ever heard. But what if it's not? What if Mom's willingness to put herself out there—to do something other than cleaning the apartment and washing her hands thirty times a day—means her problem isn't so bad after all? Besides, twenty-five thousand dollars is a lot of money. A prize like this would really help, because Mom doesn't work (except for housework, of course) and Dad pays for most things. "You should go for it," I say. "You'll definitely win."

"You think so?" Mom takes my hand. Her fingers are redder than ever and rough as sandpaper. "I never apologized for my behavior at the supermarket," she says, giving my hand a squeeze. "Or for letting you walk home alone. It was wrong of me, Kit-Kat, and I'm sorry."

If I were brave, I'd point out that sorry doesn't change the fact that she cleaned cans in public and made me wear latex gloves in front of my friends. Or that I walked home by myself when it was starting to get dark outside. I might even ask Mom why her cleaning is getting worse, and why she's so worried about germs and me getting sick. I might even admit I'm worried about her. As worried as she is about me, I'll bet.

But I'm not that brave. I also don't want to ruin this moment.

I grab a handful of popcorn and shove it in my mouth, careful not to drop any kernels on the floor. When Mom wraps her arm around me, I want to keep her next to me—and away from her vacuum—as long as possible.

8.

Sharing

The smell of gingersnaps tickles my nose when Halle and I walk into the classroom on Monday morning. Olympia is here for our second rap session and she's brought homemade cookies. I sure could use a baked good. The highlight of my weekend was helping Mom check my sheets for bedbugs. It was as if our Girls' Night reenactment never happened.

"I'd like to hear from some new rappers today," Olympia says, holding up the talking stick. "Who wants to go first?"

Kevin races over to Olympia and snatches the stick out of her hand.

"I didn't give you permission to speak, Kevin," Olympia says. "Sharing is a privilege, not a right."

"That's okay," Kevin says. "Watch this!" Before Olympia has time to stop him, Kevin puts the Burger King crown on his head and starts rapping into the talking stick:

"My name's Kevin and I'm here to say
I'm so cool in every way.
I can rap and I can rhyme.
I'm so dope, yo! It's a crime!"

Kevin bumps fists with Hector, then starts his first victory lap around the trust circle. After he's done fist-bumping the rest of us—except for Madeline, who refuses to touch him—Jane coughs into her hand. "That was quite creative, Kevin, but I don't think Olympia is inviting the fifth grade to perform *rap music*, exactly. She wants you to talk about your feelings."

Olympia sends a thank-you nod Jane's way and takes the talking stick from Kevin. She hands it to Sam, who's been waving his hand to go next.

"This may not sound like a big deal to some of you," Sam says, glancing around the trust circle, "but I have chronic eczema."

Michael's jaw drops. "Is it fatal?"

Madeline lets out a snort. "Eczema is a rash, you moron—not a life-threatening disease." She turns to Olympia. "Why are we talking about this?"

Great question.

Wilson puts down his latest medical book, *Molecular Cell Biology*, and steps forward. He's wearing a white lab coat today, with a stethoscope around his neck. Wilson wants to be a doctor when he grows up, and I'm sure he'll be a good one. He's getting plenty of practice already. "Eczema, or atopic dermatitis," Wilson tells the class, "is no laughing matter. The incessant itching can cause extreme discomfort."

"Preach," Sam says, scratching under the sleeve of his cardigan. He hands Wilson the talking stick.

Wilson bends down to examine Sam's arm. "Have you tried a steroid cream? It can be very effective."

"I don't think so," Sam says.

"You should." Wilson reaches into the pocket of his lab coat and pulls out a small white pad. "I'll write you a prescription. Date of birth?"

Olympia gets up from her seat. "Not to minimize the importance of Sam's skin condition, but let's limit the discussion to our emotions." She takes the stick from Wilson. "Who wants to go next?"

Before I can stop myself, I'm putting out my hand for the talking stick. Halle looks at me in shock, but I don't care. If I don't say this now, I never will. I take a deep breath. "How do you help someone with a problem? A problem they don't want to talk about."

Olympia pushes a stray orange braid out of her eyes. "Would you mind telling us more, Kat? If it's within your comfort zone, of course."

My problem with Mom is as far outside my comfort zone as Timbuktu, but I'll need to be more specific if I want Olympia to help me. I try again. "Someone I love has a problem. At least, I *think* it's a problem. But she—I mean, this *person*—won't admit it."

"Have you tried talking to this person about the situation?" Olympia asks. "You know, told him or her how you feel?"

"Not really," I admit. "It's too hard. Besides, this person doesn't know I'm worried."

Olympia scoots to the edge of her chair. "Talking about problems *is* hard, Kat. You're absolutely right. But guess what?"

"What?"

"If you don't talk about problems, they won't disappear on their own. They'll keep cropping up, again and again, until the problem gets bigger. And when that happens, it's that much harder to find a solution. That's why open communication is the best way forward. Does that make sense?"

It does . . . and it doesn't. Yes, keeping quiet won't make my problems with Mom go away. But what if talking about them doesn't help either? What if I tell her how I feel and she gets upset? Or worse, what if nothing changes and she *still* makes me wear latex gloves at the supermarket? All that talking would have been for nothing! Besides, I don't think Olympia realizes what I'm up against. People who clean kitchen floors with electric toothbrushes aren't your average neat freaks. Not even close.

"I don't think I can do it," I finally say. "It's a good idea, but not for me."

"How do you know unless you try?" Michael chimes in. "You can do it, Kat. You can."

Huh? Since when is Michael my personal cheerleader? I'm suddenly so embarrassed, my whole body feels itchy, as if I've caught Sam's eczema. Halle must be as surprised as I am, because her mouth is in the shape of a giant O.

As I'm processing all this, Olympia's eyes meet mine. "What if Michael is right, Kat? What if you *can* talk to this person about what's going on? How would that feel?"

I don't know, I want to tell her.

And I'm not sure if I'm ready to find out.

9.

Big News

The following Monday, I find a note waiting for me when I get home from school.

> Hi, Kit-Kat,
> Will be home around 5:30. Make yourself
> a snack. And use a plate!!!!
> Love,
> Mom ☺

I make a peanut butter and banana sandwich and take it to my room, something I can't do when Mom is home. Then I take out my phone to call Dad. I didn't speak to him all weekend, and I miss him.

"*HeWO?*" It's Henry, out of breath. He must have run for the phone. When you're three, answering the phone is as exciting as meeting Elmo.

"How goes it, bud?"

"Kitty-Kat!"

Knowing my brother is excited to hear my voice makes me smile. "I'm seeing you on Friday," I remind him. "To babysit. I'm sleeping over too."

"Yay!"

When Dad asked if I'd stay with Henry while he and Barbara ran downstairs for an early dinner with neighbors, I'd said yes right away. There'd be pizza, Dad promised, and five dollars an hour. When Halle heard about the pizza, she agreed to come too. I didn't mention the money, though. Maybe I'll surprise her and buy us fro-yo next week on the way home from school.

"Is Dad there, Hen?" I ask.

"He's on the compooter."

"Com*pu*ter," I say, repeating the word correctly, the way Dad and Barbara asked me to. "Can you put him on the phone? I want to talk to him."

"I'll have to yell."

"That's okay, bud. Go ahead."

I hear Henry take in a big breath. "Daddy!"

The minute hand on the kitchen wall clock makes a full circle before my dad gets on the phone. "Kit-Kat! Are we still on for Friday night?"

"Yeah, Dad. That's not why I called."

"Oh?"

"I need to talk to you about Mom," I say.

"What's up?" he asks.

I had planned to tell him about my idea (okay, Olympia's idea) to talk to Mom about her problem. But now that I'm about to say it out loud, it feels wrong. I go with the first thing that pops into my brain instead. "She's very happy for me because I got a ninety-eight on my French quiz," I say. "Pretty good, huh?"

"*C'est formidable*," Dad says, laughing. "You're a real French scholar."

"*Merci beaucoup.*" We chat for a few more minutes before I hang up and start my math homework. We're doing positive and negative numbers this year, which I don't understand. Dad used to help me when I was younger, but it was no use. No matter how many times he'd try to explain something to me, the concept would sail over my head like a let-go balloon. Now the math is harder, and Dad's not around to help.

Next is English, a one-page description of our assigned *Harriet the Spy* characters. I chew on my pencil, hoping for something interesting to say about The Boy with the Purple Socks. I can't think of a thing. Why does my character have to be so boring? I'd have plenty to say if I were Harriet, who spies on people and writes about them in her notebook. I mean, spying on people is *fun*. Last summer I caught the lady down the hall going to the garbage room in her underwear. I'm not sure if that counts as spying, though, because people who walk around in their underwear probably don't care who sees them. Mom won't go near the garbage room. She tips the porter extra to pick up our trash.

As I'm finishing up, I hear Mom at the door. "Where were you?" I ask, following her into the kitchen. She sets bags of Chinese takeout on the counter and goes over to the sink to wash her hands.

"I had an interview," she says, reaching for the soap. "I think it went well."

Hmmm, this is new. Mom hasn't wanted to go back to work since she lost her job as a magazine editor. I remember how Dad kept bugging her to find a new one, but Mom wasn't interested. "The magazine industry is dead," she told my dad at dinner one night. "I might as well focus my energy on something else." Too bad the "something else" turned out to be cleaning the apartment and worrying about germs.

Mom finishes her hand-washing routine, dries off on a clean dish towel, and slips on her rubber gloves. She wipes down the Chinese takeout containers before placing them on the table. "What kind of job did you interview for?" I ask once we've sat down to eat.

Mom passes me the kung pao chicken. "It wasn't for a job," she says. "I interviewed to be a contestant on *Clean Sweep*."

I almost drop the takeout container. "You're kidding."

"Nope. I didn't want to say anything until it was definite, but the producers liked my application and asked me to come in for a chat."

"About what?"

"My personal cleaning style," Mom says, reaching for the chicken. "How often I clean, which products I use . . . That kind of thing. Basically, they want to see if I'd be a good fit for the show."

A good fit? Isn't it enough that Mom wants to be on *Clean Sweep* in the first place? I can't imagine there's a line around the block for people who want to scrub toilets on TV, but you never know. "Do a lot of people audition?" I ask, curious.

"More than you'd think," Mom says. She spears a piece of broccoli. "The producers have to be selective in the screening process."

"Oh." I chew this over as I eat my chicken. I'm also wondering how many of the other contestants have a problem like Mom's. Or maybe they just want to be on TV. "Do you think they'll pick you?" I ask, picturing my mom in a sanitation worker's uniform. It's not the best image, but for twenty-five thousand dollars it's not *that* bad.

Mom serves herself more chicken. "Getting chosen is a long shot, but I think there's a good chance. I demonstrated my counter-wiping technique for the producers, and they told me I was remarkably quick and very thorough."

I look up from my food. Mom is smiling with her whole face, not just her mouth. I guess *Clean Sweep* means more to her than I realized. "I hope you get picked, Mom," I say, surprising myself by actually meaning it. "It would be cool."

"It sure would," Mom says, getting up to clear the table. "*Very* cool."

Later, I crawl into bed to read *Harriet the Spy* under the covers. I'm so wound up about *Clean Sweep*—half hoping Mom will win, half worried she won't—that I keep reading the same sentence over and over. Then I do what I couldn't do last week. I find my laptop, open my email, and click on New.

TO: Olympia.Rabinowitz@VillageHumanity.org
SUBJECT: Hello
DATE: September 25, 9:32:24 PM EDT
FROM: Kat.Greene@VillageHumanity.org

Dear Olympia,

Thank you for your advice in rap session the other day. It was very helpful. I haven't talked to the person about their problem yet (it's my mom), but I will. I'm waiting until she finds out about being on TV. It's a long story, but my mom might be on *Clean Sweep*. Have you seen it? It's a game show where people clean stuff as fast as they can. The prize is $25,000 and a lifetime supply of cleaning products. I'm glad about the money, but not so glad about the cleaning products. Cleaning is kind of like my mom's hobby, and I'm worried the show will only encourage her to do it more. Lately she can't sit, or talk, or read, or shop— or do much of anything, really—without wanting to clean something. She says she can't help it and that it calms her, but I find this hard to understand. I mean, there's nothing "calming" about cleaning. It's a lot of work!

One more thing. Okay, it's more of a question than a thing. What will happen if my mom doesn't win? I know she'll be very disappointed. I will be too.

I'm sorry if this email sounds confusing and all jumbled up, but that's how I feel right now. I wish I didn't.

Sincerely,

Kat

I reread my email. There are other things I could have told Olympia. More important things. But I'm not ready to say them, at least not yet. I close my eyes and press Send.

10.

Emails and Arm Farts

I wasn't sure she'd write back, but there's an email from Olympia in my inbox the next morning.

To: Kat.Greene@VillageHumanity.org
SUBJECT: Re: Hello
DATE: September 26 7:21:17 AM EDT
FROM: Olympia.Rabinowitz@VillageHumanity.org

Dear Kat,

    I'm glad my advice in rap session was helpful to you. And how cool that your mom might be on TV! It could be a lot of fun. At the same time, you expressed worry that your mom might not win. You said she would be very disappointed, and that you would be too.

The thing to keep in mind is that losing is always a possibility on game shows—and in life in general. But with the right attitude and proper preparation, there's a good chance your mom could walk off with the grand prize. Maybe you have other concerns about this situation you'd like to share? For instance, you mentioned how a lifetime supply of cleaning products might encourage your mom to clean more. It sounds like your mom takes cleaning very seriously. More than a hobby, maybe.

I know you haven't talked to her yet, but you may want to consider it. Talking always helps. In the meantime, if you ever feel like talking to me, you know where I am. See you in school!
Best wishes,
Olympia

I'd planned on telling Halle about Olympia's email—and about Mom's interview for *Clean Sweep*—during our walk to school. But now at our lockers while we're putting our books away, I still haven't said anything. As usual, my best friend has other things on her mind.

"Do you think Michael will ask me out?" Halle says, shoving a binder into her lock-free locker. "I'm picking up these vibes."

"Vibes?"

"I caught him looking at me in class yesterday. Twice."

"Well . . ."

The smile disappears from Halle's face. "What's that supposed to mean?"

"What?" I ask.

"You know what," she says.

"I didn't say anything!"

"Yeah, you did. You said, 'Well . . .' as in you doubt Michael will ask me out."

I feel as if I'm watching a movie I've seen a billion times before. If only I could press Fast Forward. Or better yet, Stop. "I didn't mean anything by it, Hal," I say. "It's just that I have no clue what Michael thinks. It's not like he pours his heart out to me."

"Maybe not," Halle agrees. "But he did tell everyone in rap session that he likes me."

Where does Halle get this stuff? Sure, Michael said he likes a girl who is nice, and cool, and funny. But he never said it was Halle. Now I'm wishing he had. At least it would get her to shut up and *do* something about it. Suddenly Halle grabs me by the shoulders. "I have an idea."

Oh, no. I can see where this is going, and I don't like it. Not one bit. "I'm not asking him out for you, if that's what you have in mind. Forget it."

"That's not what I was going to say," Halle replies. "Hear me out."

"Fine."

Just as Halle is about to tell me the thing I probably

don't want to hear, her eyes bug out like a TV cartoon character's. I'm surprised her tongue doesn't flop out of her mouth too. "Look," she whispers. "But don't turn around."

"How can I look without turning around?" I whisper back. "It's impossible."

"Then do it fast. And don't be obvious!"

As subtly as I can, I turn around to see what Halle's all freaked out about—and why her fingernails are now digging into my arm. It's not as bad as I thought. Michael is having a conversation with Olympia at the other end of the hall. "What's the big deal?" I ask, pulling away from Halle. "Olympia talks to kids all the time." *And writes them emails. And invites them to her office to talk.*

"I told you," Halle says, blowing out air. "He likes me."

"Just because he's talking to Olympia? He could be telling her what he had for lunch, for all you know."

"But he's not," Halle says. "Open your eyes and *look.*"

When I look again, I see that Halle's not making things up. Michael is smiling at her. When he catches us staring, he waves.

"See?" Halle says. "That's why I need you to talk to him. To find out if he likes me."

"Why can't you do it yourself?" I ask.

Halle looks at me as if I've got toilet paper stuck to my head. "You can't just go up to a boy and ask if he likes you! It's not *done* that way. How do you not know this?"

I raise my eyebrows at her.

"You know something, Kat? You really are different." Halle gives me a playful jab in the ribs. "In a good way."

"Um, thanks?"

"So, you'll do it?" Halle is smiling now.

"Do what?"

"Ask Michael if he likes me!"

"I'll think about it," I say, rubbing my sore ribs.

"Great!" Halle smiles wider. "Kat?"

"Yeah?"

"Did you know that Michael does the best arm fart? He made one before homeroom this morning and it was so realistic. You'd think he was actually *farting*."

"Halle?"

"Yeah?"

"Would you please stop talking about Michael? It's making my head hurt."

Halle gives me another playful punch. "You're funny."

No, I'm not, I think. I'm dead serious.

11.

You Can Count on Us

I'm packing my overnight bag for babysitting duty when I realize I haven't told Halle about my email from Olympia—or about Mom's decision to try out for *Clean Sweep*. I would have if she'd stopped talking about Michael long enough to listen.

Ever since she spotted Michael staring at her in the hall on Monday, Halle's become this other person. Someone I hardly know. When she's not mooning over him in class, she's talking about him at lunch and during walks to and from school. It almost makes me glad I don't have a crush. I think I'd drive myself nuts.

Mom brings me downstairs to wait for the car service Dad ordered for me and Halle. She wanted to bring us uptown in a cab herself, but Dad insisted we were old enough to go on our own. I'm glad he won the argument. I mean, who wants to be taken everywhere by their mother? Liberty is allowed to take the bus by herself, and so is Kevin. Then again, if I were Kevin's mom, I wouldn't care where he went or how he got there. I'd just be glad he was somewhere else.

"You've got everything you need?" Mom asks, scanning Thirteenth Street for the car. "Your cell charger? Clean underwear? A toothbrush?"

I almost make a joke about bringing the toothbrush she uses to clean the kitchen floor, but I stop myself in time. "I'm all set," I say, grateful to spy Halle jogging toward us with her sleeping bag. "Don't worry."

"I'm not worried," Mom says. "Just displaying the usual motherly concern."

Just then, the car pulls up to the curb. Mom motions for Halle to hurry and gives me a quick squeeze goodbye. "Text me when you get there," she says. "Don't forget."

"I won't, Mom. Promise."

Mom stands back and watches as the driver pops the trunk for our bags. "Have fun!" she calls out to us. "Wear your seat belts!"

I give her one last wave before climbing into the backseat. Halle climbs in after me and cracks the window. After I barfed on the bus last year on a field trip to the Bronx Zoo, she knows better than to trust my stomach in a moving vehicle.

"Guess what I did after school?" Halle blurts out the minute Mom's out of sight. She puts on her seat belt and makes me do the same.

"Your homework?" I say, clicking the buckle into place.

"No, silly. I Skyped with Michael for twenty-five minutes! I got to see his room and everything."

"Cool," I say.

"Michael's got a gerbil, two turtles, and a goldfish named Sylvia."

"Michael's sure got a lot of animals," I say, wishing I could have a pet. "But Sylvia? That's a strange name for a fish."

"It was his grandmother's name," Halle says, scowling. "*I* think it's cute."

Suddenly I feel my stomach lurch. To keep from getting carsick, I close my eyes and take in the familiar sounds of New York City at rush hour: the *brum-brum* of jackhammers, the screech of police sirens, voices everywhere. When the car reaches Dad's building thirty-five minutes later, my stomach and I are grateful to get out. I send Mom a quick text to let her know we're here and take the elevator with Halle up to the twelfth floor.

Barbara is waiting for us at the door. She and Dad are only going downstairs to the Morgensterns' apartment for dinner, but my stepmom looks ready to walk the red carpet. She's wearing a short sequined dress, a matching jacket, and sparkly gold jewelry. She's even got a rhinestone clip in her hair.

"Kat! Halle!" Barbara pulls us into a group hug. Her clinking bangles feel cold against the back of my neck. "I'm so glad you girls could watch Henry tonight. I was going to arrange for a sitter, but Dennis wouldn't hear of it. He said you were old enough, but—"

"But nothing," Dad says, joining us in the entrance hall. "Kat and Halle are up to the task. Right, girls? And we'll just be downstairs."

Halle offers my dad a wide grin. "That's right, Mr. Greene. You can count on us."

"Where is Henry anyway?" I ask. My brother is usually out like a shot when the doorbell rings.

"Watching TV," Dad says. "Go say hi."

I wave a quick good-bye to Dad and Barbara, grab a juice box from the fridge, and head for the family room to find Henry.

My brother is already in his pajamas, sitting cross-legged on the floor. He's surrounded by loose socks. "What are you doing?" I ask, pointing to Henry's mess. "Where did those socks come from?"

"My dwesser dwawer."

That's another thing about my brother. It takes an interpreter to figure out what he's saying. "Okay, Henry," I say slowly. "Let's put the socks away and get ready for bed."

"No!" Henry balls his chubby hands into fists. "I don't wanna go to bed. I'm not tiyood!"

A tantrum will erupt if I don't do something quick.

I run into Henry's room, grab *The Little Engine That Could*, and race back to the family room. My brother plucks the book out of my hand and presents it to Halle, Cinderella-slipper style. "Wead," he tells her.

"What do you say, Henry?" I remind him.

"Pwease."

Three read-alouds later, I'm able to peel Henry off Halle's lap and drag him to his room. After he hops into bed, I flick on his night-light and hand him Bruno, his stuffed pig. I remember when Henry first got Bruno, a gift from my mom. He was bright blue then, with big black eyes and a cute piggy snout. Now Bruno is gray and ratty and smells like feet. "Good night, bud," I say, kissing my brother's nose. Henry grabs Bruno by a raggedy ear and rolls over. I tiptoe out of the room and close the door softly behind me.

Halle wasted no time getting comfy in the family room. She's eating pizza and watching a TV cooking show. It's the one where contestants race against the clock to make meals out of bizarre ingredients like ox tongue and animal crackers. This reminds me of *Clean Sweep* and the possibility that Mom could get picked. I decide to tell Halle after she passes me the pizza box. "You won't believe this," I say, "but—"

"You talked to Michael for me!" Halle jumps up and smothers me in a bone-crushing hug. "I knew you'd come through!"

"I said I'd *think* about it," I say, untangling myself. "But that's not what I wanted to tell you."

"Oh." Halle wipes a blob of grease off her chin. "That's okay," she says, brightening. "There's no need to rush it. These things take time."

Finally my best friend may be coming to her senses. I get back to telling her about *Clean Sweep*—and my email to Olympia.

"I'm glad you emailed her," Halle says, reaching for another slice, "but what did she tell you to do about your mom?"

"Do?"

Halle frowns. "You *did* tell her how bad it's gotten, didn't you?"

"Of course I did." The lie tastes bitter in my mouth, worse than ox tongue and animal crackers combined. How can I admit to Halle that I didn't tell Olympia the whole story? That I mentioned *Clean Sweep* and not much else? She'll think I'm a big chicken. Maybe I am.

"Well, whatever Olympia said, I hope you'll tell your dad," Halle says. "He should know what's going on, Kat."

"Yeah," I say. "But once he knows the truth, he'll drag me uptown quicker than Mom can check my sheets for bedbugs."

"Then we'd never walk to school together," Halle says, "or hang out at each other's apartments whenever we feel like it."

"True," I say. "But I guess living with Dad wouldn't be the worst thing either. I mean, I like his place, and he and Barbara always make me feel at home."

"Sure, but if you actually *lived* here, they'd start using you as a built-in babysitter."

"I could order pizza all the time," I remind her. "That's a plus."

"But what about the babysitting part?" Halle asks.

I smile. We both know that a little Henry goes a long way. We drop it and get back to the cooking show.

As the winning chef is being announced, I hear a key in the lock. It's Barbara, carrying her high heels. She collapses onto the sofa and starts rubbing her feet.

"Where's my dad?" I ask.

"At the piano. He and Mindy Morgenstern were in the middle of a duet when I left."

"'Summer Nights,' from *Grease*?"

Barbara stops rubbing. "How'd you know?"

"Just a wild guess." I grin at Halle. For a middle-aged tax accountant, my dad's got a silly streak a mile wide. Combine "silly" with his "singing" and you're in for a bumpy ride.

Barbara removes her earrings and tucks her feet underneath her. "Dennis insisted on taking the Sandy part, but after a while I couldn't take it anymore. I made my excuses and came upstairs." She motions toward Henry's room. "Did you have any trouble with the little guy? He can be a real handful."

"No, Mrs. Greene," Halle says sweetly. "He was an angel."

Barbara makes a face. "That's nice of you to say, Halle, but I don't believe you for a minute. The only time Henry is an angel is when he's asleep! I'll go check on him." Barbara gets up from the couch and disappears down the hall.

At that moment Dad makes his big entrance. He's taken off his blazer and draped it over his shoulders. He reminds me of a prep-school kid in a bad eighties movie. He sings, "*Summer lovin', had me a blast. / Summer lovin' happened so fast. / Met a girl crazy for me. / Met a boy cute as can be . . .*"

Despite the look of it, Dad has not been drinking. As he likes to say, he gets "high on life." This is his way of embarrassing me without using alcohol as an excuse. He flings his blazer on the couch and takes a seat next to Halle. "So, what's the four-one-one, girls?"

I roll my eyes. "No one says that, Dad."

My father clutches his heart, stricken. "Is this true, Halle? Am I woefully behind on tween lingo?"

Halle offers an apologetic smile. "Yeah, Mr. Greene. Sorry."

I try to ignore the fact that my father has taken off his tie and looped it around his head. "Barbara told us you were singing with Mrs. Morgenstern," I say. "The Sandy part."

Dad grins, his tie flopping against his ear. "Guilty as

charged." He puffs out his chest and pretends to fluff out his nonexistent hair. Dad is as bald as Mom's hero, Mr. Clean, and he looks like him too—minus the brawny forearms and shiny gold earring.

"So," he asks, "what did you girls do while I was impressing the Morgensterns with my musical stylings? Inquiring minds want to know."

Halle giggles. "Nothing much, Mr. Greene. We read to Henry, watched TV, ate pizza. You know . . ."

"But it was fun, right?" Dad gives us a look I can't quite decipher.

"What are you getting at, Dad?" I ask.

"Okay, busted." Dad unloops the tie from his head and places it next to him on the couch. "I was hoping you girls could babysit again next weekend—or every weekend, actually. You could make it a regular gig. Like the Baby-Sitters Club."

The Baby-Sitters Club? Is Dad for real?

"I don't know, Dad," I say, looking over at Halle. "It's a big commitment."

Dad shrugs. "What can I say? I like having you here."

Or does he just like having someone here for Henry? Sometimes I'm not so sure.

12.

Let's Do This Thing

Three things happen the following week: Liberty gets her nose pierced, Wilson says he's found a cure for cancer, and Mom is offered a spot on *Clean Sweep*. I almost choke on my toaster waffle when she tells me at breakfast Friday morning.

"Why are you so surprised?" Mom asks, passing me the syrup. "You look stunned!"

I am stunned. I knew there was a chance she could get picked, but I never thought it would happen this soon. One of the contestants dropped out at the last minute, it seems, and Mom was at the top of the list. The fact that she's a New Yorker didn't hurt either. Transporting contestants to and from the city isn't cheap.

"Should we tell Dad?" I ask, drowning my waffle in maple syrup. "He'll want to know."

"You're right," Mom says. She hands me a napkin. "We should definitely tell him. Just not yet."

"Why not?"

Mom adjusts her bandanna. "No specific reason. Let's just say he won't be as enthusiastic as we are."

I suppose Mom's right. Dad won't mind the twenty-five-thousand-dollar cash prize, but seeing his ex-wife scrubbing a dirty toilet on television? Not so much. Or maybe Dad knows more about Mom's recent obsession with cleaning than she's letting on. I wish I knew.

Before I leave for school, I get my laptop to write back to Olympia. I never answered her last email, and I feel kind of bad.

TO: Olympia.Rabinowitz@VillageHumanity.org
SUBJECT: News
DATE: October 6 7:47:19 AM EDT
FROM: Kat.Greene@VillageHumanity.org

Dear Olympia,

    Guess what? My mom got picked for *Clean Sweep*. She told me at breakfast this morning. I want to tell my dad, but Mom thinks we should wait. She's probably right. Still, I wish I could tell him.
    See you in school,
    Kat

I try to share my big news with Halle on the walk to school, but I don't get a chance: Michael has started using Axe body spray. In Halle's world, this is more important than the discoveries of gravity and electricity combined.

Now, in art, she's giving me the latest update—proof that Michael likes her. "I can see it in his eyes," Halle says, pulling a smock over her head. "He's always, well, *blinking* at me, and you know what that means."

Yeah, I think. *He probably has an eye infection.*

I try to concentrate on the still life in front of me— three rotting clementines in a cracked turquoise bowl— but it's hard. The sickly-sweet fruit smell is so disgusting, I'm worried my toaster waffle will come in for a landing on the art-room floor.

"He's going to ask me out," Halle says, squinting at the clementines. "If not this week, definitely next. No thanks to you, by the way."

"What's that supposed to mean?"

"Just what I said."

I put down my paintbrush. "I never agreed to talk to him, Hal, and you know it. Why can't you get it through your head? If you'd only listen, you'd see that—"

"*Shhhh!* Quiet back there!" It's our art teacher, Remy, yelling at us from behind her easel. Remy is a Village Calamity celebrity. She's been at the school forever (she taught my *mom*), and it's common knowledge that she poses nude for a drawing class at the Art Students League. I feel sorry for the poor, unsuspecting art students who have to see Remy naked. She's not exactly the Mona Lisa.

Remy steps away from her easel and starts circling the room. "Representational accuracy is meaningless in the creation of art," she tells the class, spitting out each word like a lemon seed. "It's the emotional intensity that counts!" She strides over to Liberty. "This," she declares, holding up Liberty's painting, "emits true feeling. *Passion!*"

I wish I could say the same about my work of art. Despite my best efforts, my clementines look like rotten tomatoes, all squished and lumpy. "Where's the emotion, Katrina?" Remy asks when she gets to my table. "I don't see it anywhere! I expect more from you." She *tsks-tsks* and moves on to Wilson, who's wiping blue paint off his lab coat.

I'm so mad, I could scream. Not because Remy insulted my painting, or even that she called me by my given name, Katrina. I'm annoyed that my teacher probably expects me to be as talented as my mom, Class Artist of 1989. If only Remy knew the truth: that the only brush my mom uses now is to clean the toilet.

Later that day Jane makes us sit in our *Harriet the Spy* pairs. I'm squeezed in a corner with Sam, praying for the hands of the clock to spring to 2:45 p.m., dismissal time. Sam interrupts my wishful thinking. "We should work on the Harriet project this weekend, Kat. We've only got seven weeks until the Thanksgiving assembly."

"Seven weeks is a long time," I say. "Besides, I've been doing a lot of work on my own. That's got to count for something."

Sam cracks his knuckles. "I'm glad you're on top of things, Kat, but there's no need to fly solo. We're a team."

"Yeah, but—" I scramble for an excuse. "I have to babysit my little brother this weekend. I promised my stepmom."

This is not exactly true. I did tell Barbara I might be free to watch Henry on Saturday afternoon for a couple of hours while she and Dad go to the movies. But I never made any cross-my-heart-and-hope-to-die promises. Now I wish I had.

"Wait!" Sam holds up his hand like a traffic cop. "I could babysit with you. I know a lot about kids. My sister, Chloe, is almost five and I watch her all the time."

"Well, I—"

"Or better yet, I could bring Chloe with me. She can play with your brother while we work on the project. It'll be perfect." Sam offers me a face-cracking grin. "Let's do this thing!"

"I don't know," I say, picturing Henry and Sam's little sister destroying Dad and Barbara's apartment faster than a wrecking ball. "How would we get any work done? You can't leave two little kids alone. They need to be supervised."

"Elmo," Sam says simply. "I don't know about your little brother, but Chloe can watch *Sesame Street* all day."

"Henry's mom might not like that," I say, thinking fast. "She prefers him to play games or read books. You know, educational stuff."

"I doubt a couple of hours of *Sesame Street* will do any harm, Kat. Come on. We don't want to bomb the Harriet project. It's important."

Sam's got a point. "Okay, Saturday afternoon," I say. "But only for a couple of hours."

"Sweet!" Sam leans over to give me a high five.

Yeah, I think, high-fiving him back.

Sweet.

13.

Unanswered Questions

Mom is sterilizing the silverware when I walk into the kitchen the next morning. "I need to work on my cleaning speed for the show," she says, dropping a handful of spoons into a large pot of boiling water. "I'm not fast enough. I'm thinking of using a timer, but that may be overkill. What do you think?"

"Good morning to you too."

"Sorry, Kit-Kat." Mom blows me a kiss as she heads for the sink. She turns on the water and starts lathering up. "I'm just nervous about the show," she says, reaching for more hand soap, "and meeting some of the other local Sweepers at dinner tonight."

Oh, yeah. Tonight's the night Mom is getting together with the other *Clean Sweep* contestants, or

"Sweepers," to prepare for the show. Before the show tapes at the end of October, the producers wanted everybody to meet for dinner at a fancy French restaurant on the Upper East Side. I hope a fight doesn't break out over who gets to do the dishes.

I grab some OJ from the fridge and sit down at the breakfast bar. "How do you know you're not fast enough?" I ask, waiting for Mom to get me a glass. "You haven't seen the other contestants yet."

"True." Mom says. "But if I want to win, I have to be the best."

"You *are* the best, Mom. I mean, look at this place. The floor's so clean, you can lick it!"

Mom laughs as she leans over to pour my juice. When she's done, she puts on her rubber gloves and reaches for a bottle of Fantastik. "Aren't you supposed to go to your dad's later?" she says, aiming the nozzle at the countertop. "To work on the Harriet project with Sam?"

"Thanks for reminding me."

"Oh, come on. What's the problem—the project or Sam?"

"Both," I say. "I didn't get picked for Harriet, and Sam is kind of annoying. He's also obsessed with"—I make air quotes with my fingers—"'getting ahead of the competition.' It's so dumb."

Mom rips off a paper-towel square and starts mopping up the cleanser. "You won't always get the lead in plays, honey. But I think you already know that."

I do. Olympia said pretty much the same thing in her email—how losing is always a possibility, on game shows and in life in general. But that doesn't make it any easier.

"And don't forget," Mom adds, "you could do a lot worse than Sam. When I was at Village Humanity, this boy named Jimmy Vincent took a Polaroid of his behind during a class trip to Bear Mountain. He made a bunch of photocopies and handed them out to every kid in the class."

I can't help but smile. "Did he get in trouble?"

Mom squirts more cleanser on the countertop and rips off another paper-towel square. "Remy said he had a flair for photography and encouraged him to sign up for after-school classes. Can you imagine?"

Actually, I can.

As I watch my mom clean an already-clean counter, it occurs to me that now would be the perfect time to take Olympia's advice and talk to her about her problem. I don't want to make her angry, so I choose my words carefully.

"I was wondering about something . . ."

Mom looks up from the counter. "Yes?"

"Well . . ." I pause. "Why do you clean so much lately? You're always doing it. Washing your hands too."

Mom's jaw muscle twitches. "Lots of people do that. It's not a crime."

"I never said it was. I was just wondering."

"Oh." Mom finds a pair of metal tongs from the canister on the counter and goes over to the stove. Then she starts removing the silverware from the pot of boiling water, piece by piece. First the spoons, then the forks, then the knives. Before long, a silvery line of cutlery has snaked its way across the countertop.

"Mom? I asked you a question."

She reaches for a clean dish towel and starts drying the silverware. First the spoons, then the forks, then the knives . . .

"Mom?" I say again. "Aren't you going to answer?"

Mom spins around. Her bandanna is on crooked and fraying at the edges. "It calms me, Kat. I can't explain it—I'm sorry. There's nothing else to say."

But you can try, I feel like telling her. Problems don't disappear on their own. But Mom is in no mood for talking. If anything, she looks sad, like when I'm home sick with a fever and she's waiting for my temperature to go down. I want to say something, but it's useless. She's already back at the stove.

I storm off to my room and flop down on my bed. I listen to the radiator hiss. Boy, is it loud—and *hot*. I get up and crack the window. Cold air whooshes in and tickles the tip of my nose. I close it again. Then I start counting cabs. I get to thirty-seven before I feel bored.

But it's not boredom I feel, flopping back on the bed. I'm *mad*. Why can't Mom answer my question?

And tell me why she cleans so much, and why she's so afraid of germs? It wouldn't have killed her. I stare at the fuzzy peace-sign rug next to my bed, remembering how Mom washed it herself *and* had it dry-cleaned before allowing it inside my room. It came from a flea market, and I was surprised she let me keep it at all.

I should be thinking about what Sam and I will talk about later, when we meet at Dad's. But how can I concentrate on the Harriet project when I'm this upset? When I want answers and Mom won't give them to me? I reach for my laptop and bring up Google.

I type in "people who clean all the time" and wait for my choices. An article called "How to Stop Obsessive Cleaning" pops up at the top of the page. I skim through it until the following sentence catches my eye: "Obsessive cleaning may be symptomatic of wider anxieties, such as fear of contamination."

Well, that makes sense, I think, remembering Mom's comments about the germs on my backpack and on the handle of the shopping cart. The Purell in her purse. The antibacterial wipes. The latex gloves. I keep reading.

"People who clean compulsively wish they could stop, but they feel as if they must do so in order to prevent catastrophe and illness."

My heart starts pounding. When Mom said she couldn't help it, she wasn't exaggerating. Clearly this cleaning thing is beyond her control. Plus she's always worried I'll get sick. Does that mean something is wrong with her? Or is she just a neat freak like she always says? I type in "neat freak" and find this:

"The main difference between 'neat freaks' and people with OCD is that 'neat freaks' like being neat. People with OCD wish they weren't that way."

There's that word, OCD. I've heard it before and I think I know what it means. I need to be sure, though—especially if there's a chance Mom's got it. I type in: "What is OCD?" and within seconds I find a definition.

"Obsessive-Compulsive Disorder (OCD) is a common, chronic, and long-lasting anxiety disorder in which a person has uncontrollable, reoccurring thoughts (*obsessions*) and behaviors (*compulsions*) that he or she feels the urge to repeat over and over. Examples include checking the door multiple times to make sure it's really locked or washing your hands until they're scrubbed raw."

Wait.

Washing your hands until they're scrubbed raw . . .

I picture Mom's hands, all red and cracked and lobstery. Then I reread the words on the screen. But what am I supposed to *do* with these words?

I wish I knew.

14.

Study Session

Part of me wants to email Olympia and ask her to explain what I read online. The other part wants to pretend I never heard of OCD in the first place. It seems weird, and scary, and very, *very* serious. I know I could ask Dad about it, but he's never mentioned OCD before and I don't want to put any ideas in his head. Besides, I know what he'll say: "Come live uptown with me!" But that's not something I'd ever want to do, no matter how many times he asks.

I'll write to Olympia later, I decide, after I've had time to think about things. For now, I've got to get ready for my study session with Sam. I throw on jeans and a long-sleeved T-shirt, snatch my jacket from the hall closet, and go into the kitchen to get Mom. She insisted on taking me to Dad's in a cab herself, even though I told her it's babyish. I guess you can't win every battle.

I find her at the kitchen counter, a paper towel in one hand and her phone in the other. She smiles when she sees me. "I'm using the timer to increase my cleaning speed," Mom says, holding up her phone. "Great idea, don't you think?"

If she wants to know what I *really* think, I'd say the timer is fine but maybe she should work harder at talking to me. But that's not what she wants to hear. I'm not even sure that's what I want to say. I tell her to get her coat so we can go.

There's little traffic on the FDR Drive, so we get to Dad's in record time: twenty-five minutes from door to door. Mom waves good-bye from the back seat of the cab rather than taking me upstairs. She's still in her cleaning clothes, but that's not it. I'm pretty sure she doesn't want to see Dad. My parents get along fine, but some things—like coming face-to-face with Dad's happy second family—are just too hard. I get it.

Before I can show Dad the French quiz I forgot to bring with me last week, or even say hi to Barbara and Henry, who are playing Candy Land in the family room, the doorbell rings. It's Sam and Chloe, ten minutes early.

"Nice place you have here, Mr. Greene," Sam says, stepping into the entrance hall. "Do you own or rent?" He hands Dad his jacket and beckons to Chloe to follow him inside.

Dad raises an eyebrow at me, but I just shrug. If he wants to answer Sam's nosy question, that's up to him.

"Well, we were renting before the building went co-op," Dad says, still holding Sam's jacket, "but then, with the favorable mortgage rates, we figured we might as well put in an offer."

"You didn't pay the asking price, I hope?" Sam is frowning now.

"Oh, no. Way below. We got a good deal, actually."

"That's good to hear, sir. Well played."

"Thanks." Dad is trying not to smile.

Sam gestures to his little sister. She's picking her nose with her pinkie. "This is Chloe."

Chloe takes off her yellow slicker and drops it on the floor. "Do you have Barbies?" she asks me.

"Um, I don't think so, Chloe," I say, trying to ignore the finger rammed up her nose. "My brother, Henry, has other toys to play with, though. Want to go into the family room and see?"

Chloe nods and inches closer to me. I should take her hand, I realize. That's what nice people do. But I don't feel like being nice. I feel like dousing Chloe's hands in Purell, starting with her pinkie. If only I'd taken one of Mom's extra bottles.

Barbara appears and kneels down to Chloe's level. "I'm Barbara," she says, putting her arm around the little girl's shoulders. "Henry's mom, and Kat's stepmom."

"Stepmom?" Chloe's eyes bug out in alarm. "Like in *Cinderella?* She's mean!"

I want to laugh, but I feel bad for Barbara. I duck down too. "Barbara is nothing like the stepmom in *Cinderella*, Chloe. She's a nice stepmom. The best!" I lean over and give Barbara a hug.

"I owe you one," Barbara whispers to me before grabbing Chloe's hand and leading her down the hall.

Later, when the grown-ups have left, I go into the family room to check on Henry and Chloe. They're squished together in front of the TV, watching Big Bird count to ten in Spanish. I hand each kid a sippy cup and a box of raisins and head for the dining room to find Sam. He's already at the table, flipping through a spiral notebook. We decide to start with The Boy with the Purple Socks.

"'What is the significance of this character?'" Sam reads off the directions sheet. "'Back up your answer with concrete examples.'"

"That's easy," I say. "The Boy with the Purple Socks is new to the school, which makes him an outsider. Harriet feels like an outsider too, when her friends read her notebook and get mad at her for all the mean things she wrote about them."

Sam scratches his chin. "I don't know if I agree with you, Kat. Harriet didn't say anything mean. She was just being honest. Her classmates shouldn't have looked at the notebook. It's their own fault they got hurt."

"Well, sure," I say, "but people do things they're not supposed to do all the time. Think about it, Sam. If I had a diary lying around and you found it, wouldn't you take a look?"

Sam crosses his arms over his skinny chest. "I would not. I would respect your privacy."

"That's what you say now. But what if the diary was out in the open? You know, on a table or something? Chances are, you'd read it."

"Nope." Sam shakes his head. "That would be an invasion of Kat World."

Kat World? "Let's move on," I say, tapping the directions sheet. "Read."

Sam starts reciting the next question, his voice high and squeaky. "'How has this character changed throughout the course of the novel? As above, back up your argument with concrete examples.'"

I rack my brain for ways The Boy with the Purple Socks changes, but I can't think of a thing. He's too boring to change. I tell this to Sam.

Sam puts down his chewed-up pencil. "The Boy with the Purple Socks changes significantly by the end of the novel. Not only does he allow the Spy Catcher Club to borrow his purple socks, but he also wears *green* ones during the club's parade. For another thing . . ."

While Sam is blabbing on about how The Boy with the Purple Socks has changed when I know he really hasn't, I start counting the days until this stupid project is over. I like *Harriet the Spy* as much as the next person, and I even like Sam. But with everything going on with Mom lately, it's hard to care about purple socks. Or green ones.

"Kat?" Sam leans in closer. "I really like you."

"I like you too, Sam, and I like this book. I'm just having a hard time liking The Boy with the Purple Socks. He doesn't really do much."

Sam grins, revealing a flash of blue tooth elastics. He puts down the directions sheet. "We're a lot like Sport and Harriet, you know."

"Um, that was random. What do you mean, Sam?"

"Well, Harriet isn't like everybody else. She does her own thing, without caring what people think. You're the same way, Kat. You're different. I mean, look at your hairstyle. You still wear pigtails."

I touch one of my pigtails. I never gave my hair much thought. I just like the style because it's easy. But now that Sam's pointed it out, I worry that pigtails are weird or babyish.

"And I'm like Sport," Sam continues. "He isn't afraid to tell Harriet how he feels about things—like admitting his father sleeps all day and his mother ran away with all the money."

"So?" I ask. "What's your point?"

Sam's smile gets bigger. "I feel as if I can tell *you* anything, Kat. Anything at all."

"That's, um, good to know, Sam, but can we please get back to The Boy with the Purple Socks?"

As I'm reaching for the directions sheet, Sam comes closer and squinches up his eyes. Before I know what's happening, I feel a pair of squishy Sam lips on mine. *Blech*! Sam Teitelbaum is kissing me!

I leap out of my seat. "What are you *doing?*"

"I'm sorry, Kat. I couldn't help myself."

"Oh, yes, you could!" I'm shouting now, but I don't care. I point in the direction of the family room. "Go get your sister and leave. Now!"

Sam hangs his head. "I said I was sorry. Don't make such a big deal out of it. I wanted to show you how much I like you—that's all."

"And I want you out of my house!"

"Okay, okay. I'm going." Sam slinks off to the family room and returns with Chloe.

"I didn't get to play Barbies," she says, clutching her box of raisins.

If I were in the mood to care, I'd say something like, "That's too bad, Chloe," or "Maybe next time." But why lie? There will be no next time.

I open the front door and watch as Sam and his little sister step into the hallway. As I'm closing the door behind them, Sam appears in the open crack. "I'd like our jackets," he says stiffly. "And my directions sheet."

I flounce over to the closet and grab the jackets. "Here!" I yell. "Take them!"

"And the directions sheet?"

In reply, I slam the door in his face.

15

More Than You Think

I watch *Sesame Street* with Henry until Dad and Barbara get back. When Dad asks how it went with Sam, I roll my eyes. Dad seems to get it, because he doesn't say more. He just asks if I'm ready for him to bring me home.

I'm surprised to find Mom standing inside her walk-in closet when I walk into her room. I'm even more surprised to see her at the full-length mirror, trying on clothes. Shirts, sweaters, jeans, dresses, and a jumble of shoes and boots are scattered on the floor. I repeat: *scattered on the floor.*

"Whoa, Mom. What's going on?"

Mom bends down to pick up some sweaters and carries them over to her bed. "I've got nothing to wear for the *Clean Sweep* dinner," she says, reaching for a navy V-neck to fold. "People say that all the time, but for me it's true. I haven't got a single thing!" Mom flops down on the bed. I flop down next to her.

"Want to borrow something of mine?" I ask. "I've got lots of nice stuff you could wear."

Mom leans over and plants a mushy kiss on my cheek. "Thanks, Kit-Kat, but you and I aren't exactly the same size."

Mom's got a point. She's short and weighs as much as a large fourth grader. I'm built more like Dad: tall, with a bit of extra weight around my middle. Grandma Belle calls it puppy fat, which I don't exactly appreciate. "Why don't we go shopping?" I suggest, propping a pillow behind my head. "There's plenty of time before your dinner. It'll be fun!"

Mom glances at the clock on her nightstand. "We could, but I don't have the energy. I'm sure I can dig up something."

I picture the contents of Mom's closet: out-of-date office clothes, faded overalls, and a grubby red bandanna. "Macy's has a good selection," I say, not ready to give up. "And it's open until nine thirty."

Mom looks up, surprised. "How on earth did you know that?"

"I know more than you think," I say, getting up from the bed. I want to tell her about Sam's barfy kiss, but it might put her over the edge. Kissing equals germs, and germs equal more worry for Mom. Instead, I say the project is going well and head to my room to text Halle.

> Are you there?

What's up?

> You'll never guess

????

> Sam kissed me!!

YUCK!!!!!!

> Ikr!

You ok?

> I'm super grossed out

Boil your mouth

> Good idea

Wish MM would kiss ME!

> Lol

Ttyl

> Cu

The more I think about Sam's squidgy lips pressed up against mine, the sicker I feel. Not only was the actual kiss disgusting, but I was hoping my first one would be with someone special, in the back of a horse-drawn carriage in Central Park, maybe, or by the fountain at Lincoln Center. Not with Sam Teitelbaum in my dad's apartment.

I'm deciding whether to tell Olympia about Sam—or to ask about OCD, which I still don't understand—when Mom stops by my room. She's ready for the Sweepers' dinner and feels funny about leaving me alone. "Are you sure you don't want to stay at your dad's?" she asks for what feels like the bazillionth time. "I'll drop you off on the way."

I sigh. "We've been over this before, Mom. I'm old enough to stay by myself. You can trust me."

Mom yanks a loose thread off her skirt. "Trust has nothing to do with it, Kit-Kat. I'm just worried about your safety."

After I promise not to set the house on fire, drown in the bathtub, or open the door to strangers, Mom seems convinced. Then she asks what I think of her outfit. "Are the pearls too much?" she asks, pointing to her neck.

I shake my head. They were a gift from Dad on Mother's Day. I was six. I remember how Mom gasped when she opened the black velvet box. "They're gorgeous, Dennis!" she squealed, fastening the clasp at the back of her neck. "I'm never taking them off." And she didn't. She wore her pearls every day, even to the grocery store. Dad thought she was being silly, but Mom didn't care. She loved her pearls.

Now, as Mom is standing in front of me, wearing the necklace she loved but hasn't worn in forever, I give her my honest opinion. "You look great, Mom. Very pretty." It's nice to see her out of her cleaning clothes for a change.

Mom motions for me to duck down so she can reach my cheek to kiss it. "I remember when you were small enough for *me* to duck down," she says, gazing at our shared reflection in the mirror. "When did you get so tall?"

When you were sterilizing the silverware.

Or wiping down cans at the supermarket.

Or checking my sheets for bedbugs.

But I don't say any of this. I just smile, and let my cheek be kissed.

✧

After Mom has left the apartment and made sure I locked the door behind her, I microwave some leftover spaghetti and bring it to my room. I eat watching a video of a cute Siamese kitten trying to jump out of a ski boot. Eventually he gets tired and gives up. Poor cute kitty.

I remember how I begged Mom for a cat after my parents divorced. "I don't have brothers or sisters," I said. "I need a friend."

"Humans aren't meant to live with animals," Mom told me, wrinkling up her nose. "It's unsanitary."

I knew better than to argue.

When I'm done eating, I go into my closet and take out the old coffee can with my Snapple cap collection inside. Not counting the one about humans sharing fifty percent of their DNA with bananas (I gave it to Halle), I've got fifty-three caps. Not bad, considering I've been collecting them for only two years. I sort through the caps until I find my favorites.

Real Fact #126: A pigeon's feathers are heavier than its bones.

Real Fact #941: In South Korea, it is against the rules for a professional baseball player to wear cabbage leaves inside of his hat.

Real Fact #444: The Statue of Liberty wears a size 879 sandal.

Real Fact #50: Mosquitoes have 47 teeth.

I'd love to know how the Snapple people came up with the last one. I mean, how do you count a mosquito's teeth? They're so tiny! So tiny, there's no way you can brush them. Mosquitos must have very bad breath, I decide. Worse than Halle's in homeroom after an onion bagel.

I put my caps back in the coffee can and get out *Harriet the Spy*. I open to the part where Harriet is rolling around on the living-room floor, pretending to be an onion. Too bad The Boy with the Purple Socks doesn't get to roll around like an onion. That could be fun.

After I've read for a while, my eyelids begin to feel heavy. I change into my pajamas, brush my teeth, and climb into bed. I'm drifting off to sleep when I realize that the coffee can is still next to my bed. If I don't put it back in the closet, I could trip over it at night when I get up to pee. But my eyelids feel heavier, and heavier . . .

Before I know it, the morning light is streaming through my bedroom window.

16.

Spring Cleaning

I'm still in bed when I hear the noise.

Clink-clink CLANK!

Clink-clink CLANK!

I wander into the kitchen to investigate.

Mom is standing at the open refrigerator, a black garbage bag at her feet. She's tossing out bottles of salad dressing, and other stuff too. Tubs of butter, jars of jam. Pickles, mustard, mayonnaise. "Why are you cleaning the fridge so early?" I ask. "It's not even seven o'clock!"

Mom tries to laugh, but it sounds like she's got a chicken bone stuck in her throat. "I'm doing a bit of spring cleaning—that's all." She gives me a tight smile and tugs at her bandanna.

"Spring cleaning? It's the beginning of October, Mom."

"I know, but it can't hurt to get a head start. Right?"

So *not* right.

I go to the bathroom and brush my teeth. When I come back, Mom is still at it. "How was the dinner with the Sweepers last night?" I ask, drying my hands on my pajamas. "Were they nice?" I get a carton of OJ from the fridge and plunk down at the breakfast bar. After Mom hands me a glass, she pulls out a stack of plates and places them in a large cardboard box. I narrow my eyes. "What are you doing?"

"The same thing I've been doing all morning," Mom says, sealing the box with packing tape. "Spring cleaning." She puts "spring" in air quotes this time.

"But that's your wedding china!"

Mom brushes off her hands. "True. But you know the saying 'Out with the old and in with the new'? Well, that's what I'm doing. Tossing out the old to make way for something new. It's very therapeutic. But don't worry. I'm giving the good stuff to Goodwill."

"I'm not worried about *that*," I say. "I just think it's weird that you're giving away our stuff."

Mom looks up from her packing. "Don't you have homework to do?"

"I did it last night while you were out."

"Then why don't you help me? I could use an extra pair of hands."

I don't want to help Mom toss out her wedding china. It's off-white, with tiny rosebuds around the edges. When I was little, she'd let me use it for tea parties with my stuffed animals. She made tiny sandwiches and everything.

And then I see it, in the corner of the kitchen. A cardboard box with my Snapple cap collection in it. Mom must have snuck the coffee can out of my room while I was sleeping—or maybe even a few minutes ago, when I was brushing my teeth. I *knew* I should have put it back in my closet! "What's my coffee can doing in that box?" I ask.

"It's garbage, Kat. Just an old can filled with bottle caps."

"They're *Snapple* caps," I correct her, "and I've been collecting them since third grade!"

"Collecting them?" Mom stops packing. "Not off the street, I hope."

"Well, yeah," I admit. "And other places too. But I always wash them off first."

Mom sucks in her breath. "I don't care. Those caps are crawling with germs. You could get sick."

"No, I couldn't," I say. "I used soap. And bleach." This is not true, but what Mom doesn't know won't hurt her.

"Forget it," Mom says, picking up the box. "This is going into the trash. *Now.*"

I get up and pull the box away from her. "It's my stuff, and it's not going anywhere."

"That's it," Mom says. "To your room."

Mom may want me to go to my room, but I have other plans. I put down the box and start digging through it. My Snapple cap collection, I discover, is not the only thing Mom wants to throw away. My peace-sign rug is in there too. "You can't be serious," I say, trying to keep my voice calm. "You know I love this rug!"

Mom sighs. "You shouldn't be so attached to possessions, Kat. They're just things."

"I like my things," I say quietly.

Olympia had told me to talk to Mom. To share my feelings and try to understand how she feels. I tried that and it didn't work. Now I can see why. It's impossible to talk to someone who doesn't understand how *I* feel. Someone who would throw out my favorite things without thinking twice.

Anger slams into me like a bumper car. How dare Mom treat my feelings as if they don't matter. As if I don't matter. Well, forget that. I pick up the box and march down the hall to my room.

"Where do you think you're going?" Mom yells after me. She storms over and tries to pull the box out of my hands. "Give it to me, Kat. I mean it."

"Make me!"

Mom tries again, gripping both sides of the box and tugging hard. I lose my balance and stumble backward, slamming into the wall. "You almost knocked me over!" I yell, still holding the box. "What's *wrong* with you?"

Mom covers her mouth with her hands. "I'm so sorry, Kat! I don't know what came over me. These things make me feel so uneasy."

I'm sorry she feels that way, but trying to trash my Snapple cap collection and then almost knocking me over? That's too much!

With the box still in my hands, I run to my room and quickly get dressed. Then I dump the caps into a plastic bag and toss it in my backpack, along with my laptop, my phone, and the twenty-dollar bill Mom gave me for emergencies. It's too early to go to Halle's, but the diner on Seventh Avenue is open twenty-four hours. I grab my backpack and head out the front door without closing it behind me. Let our neighbors see our dirty laundry.

See if I care.

17.

Maybe Even Worse

Despite the early hour, the Starlight Diner is packed with hungry customers when I walk in. I take a seat at the counter and give the waitress my order: two glazed donuts and a chocolate milk shake. Mom doesn't like me having sweets in the morning, but she's not here to stop me.

At seven forty-five, it occurs to me that I should tell Olympia what's going on. She might not have all the answers, but at least she can listen to me. I pull out my laptop and log in to my school email account.

TO: Olympia.Rabinowitz@VillageHumanity.org
SUBJECT: Coming clean
DATE: October 8, 7:47 AM EDT
FROM: Kat.Greene@VillageHumanity.org

Dear Olympia,

    I took your advice and tried talking to my mom. It didn't go very well. She got mad and yelled at me. This morning she tried to throw out some of my stuff, including my Snapple cap collection. I wouldn't let her, though. I put the caps in a bag to give to Halle for safekeeping. I didn't have time to save my favorite rug, unfortunately. It came from a flea market in Chelsea, and I'll never find another one like it.

    There's something else I should tell you. I'm not sure how to put this, but I've been leaving out a lot of important information in my emails. For one thing, you guessed right when you said my mom's cleaning is more than a hobby. It's pretty much her full-time job. She washes her hands a lot too.

I look up from my email. Should I tell Olympia that I Googled OCD and think Mom's got it? I could, but I don't know that for sure. I mean, I *think* she's got it, but I'm not a doctor. Instead, I sign my email and hit Send. Then I gobble up the rest of my sugary breakfast and get up to leave for the only place I want to be right now.

❧

Halle's hair is spread out like a curly brown halo when I walk into her room ten minutes later. "Hal?" I say, giving her a little poke. "You awake?"

Halle opens a sleepy eye. "Kat?" She sits up slowly. "What are you doing here?"

"Your mom let me in." Mrs. Maklansky didn't say a word when I showed up at her doorstep at ten after eight. She just pointed to a box of Cheerios on the kitchen counter and shuffled back to bed.

I kick off my shoes and scooch in next to Halle. I tell her about Mom's cleaning spree and how she tried to throw my stuff in the trash. I save Mom's box-grabbing freak-out for last.

Halle wakes up immediately. "Your Mom *pushed* you? I can't believe it."

"She didn't do it on purpose," I explain. "She was trying to grab the box out of my hands and I fell."

"Still." Halle pushes a stray curl out of her eye. "Moms aren't supposed to do stuff like that."

"She was mad about the Snapple caps, I guess. You know . . . all those 'scary' germs." I roll my eyes. "They can kill you if you're not careful."

Halle shoots me a sympathetic smile. "You need to tell your dad what's going on, Kat. You really do."

"I know." I lie back and stare up at the ceiling. It's still dotted with the glow-in-the-dark stars I helped Halle put up when she was afraid of the dark.

Halle props herself up on her elbows. "You think your dad will be mad?"

"Mad that my mom tried to throw away my things?"

"Well, yeah, and mad that you didn't tell him about your mom's problem sooner."

What Halle doesn't say—and what we both know is

true—is that Mom's problem is getting worse. Wrestling me to the ground over an old coffee can proves it. But if I tell Dad what happened, he'll make me live uptown with him and Barbara for sure—no questions asked. Still, I can't pretend everything is fine forever. As Olympia said in rap session, problems don't go away on their own.

"I'll talk to my dad," I promise Halle. "The next time I see him. I swear."

"Girl Scout's honor?"

"We're not Girl Scouts," I say.

"You know what I mean." Halle bounces out of bed to get dressed. She turns around. "Kat?"

"Yeah?"

"This may not be the best time to bring this up, but did you notice how Michael was staring at me in the cafeteria on Friday? I was biting into my grilled cheese, when I looked up and saw . . ."

Leave it to Halle to talk about her crush in a crisis. My best friend's got it bad.

I smile for the first time all day.

18.

Sushi Means Sorry

Mom is vacuuming the window blinds when I get home later that afternoon. She stops when she sees me. "Halle's mom called to tell me where you were," she says, trying to catch my eye. "She didn't want me to worry."

I shrug and head for my room. The silent treatment is the least she deserves.

There's a letter waiting for me on my desk. I recognize the handwriting right away. It's from Mom.

Dear Kit-Kat,
I can't apologize enough for my disgraceful behavior this morning. I was upset and took it out on you. I am so, so sorry.
I know you're not ready to forgive me,

but maybe after you've had time to think things over, you could consider accepting my apology? Again, I am so sorry for how I acted and for taking your belongings. It will never happen again.
Love,
Mom

P.S. Your rug is at the dry cleaner's. I promise to return it.

Mom is right about one thing. I *don't* feel like accepting her apology. Not now, and maybe not ever. Thank goodness I left my Snapple caps with Halle. At least I know they're safe.

I get out my laptop and see two emails in my inbox. One is from Jane, reminding us to bring in our Harriet questions on Monday. The other is from Olympia. I'm surprised she wrote back on a Sunday, when teachers have better things to do with their time.

TO: Kat.Greene@VillageHumanity.org
SUBJECT: Re: Coming clean
DATE: October 8 12:07:16 PM EDT
From: Olympia.Rabinowitz@VillageHumanity.org

Dear Kat,
    Thank you for sharing your thoughts and feelings

about your mom's problem. I'm sorry to hear that she tried to throw out your things. This couldn't have been easy for you.

I don't mean to push, but again, if you ever want to come by for a chat, my door is always open.

All my best,

Olympia

"Kat?" Mom is standing at my door with a takeout menu. "I was thinking of ordering sushi for lunch. Is that okay?"

Ordering takeout—i.e., accepting food from strangers with potentially unwashed hands—is Mom's way of saying sorry. I'm not in a forgiving mood, but resisting my favorite food is not something I'm willing to do, no matter how mad I am. "Sushi's great," I say, snapping my laptop shut.

Mom inches closer. "What are you working on?"

I search my mental hard drive for a little white lie. If Mom sees Olympia's email, I'm toast. "I'm doing, uh . . . research. For school."

"Oh?" Mom adjusts the strap of her overalls. "What kind of research?"

"For um . . . the Harriet project. I want to be prepared."

"Good strategy." Mom goes over to my bed and starts smoothing down my comforter. When she looks up, her eyes are sad. "I need to tell you why I was so upset this morning."

I'm listening . . .

"I'm dropping out of the show."

"What?" This is not the confession I was expecting to hear. "What happened?"

Mom leans over to plump up my pillow. "Well, in exchange for the grand prize, the winning contestant is required to appear in national advertising campaigns and TV commercials. It says so in the contract—and there's no getting out of it. I tried."

"Why would you want to get out of it?" I ask. "Being in a commercial sounds like fun. It's better than cleaning the house all day, that's for sure."

Mom frowns.

"That's not what I meant." I start again. "I mean, you shouldn't quit because you're scared. You and Dad tell me that all the time."

"I know." Mom brushes some lint off my comforter. "I didn't realize what I was getting myself into. It's a huge responsibility and I'm not ready to commit to so much."

"What are you going to do?"

"Besides go into the kitchen to order our sushi?" Mom gets up from the bed. "I wish I knew."

I wish I did too. The one thing that got her excited for the first time in ages is now a no-go.

19.

If You Have Something to Say, Say It

"Are you *sure* I can't change?" It's the Monday after the Kissing Incident and I'm standing at Jane's desk, begging for a new Harriet partner. My classmates are at lunch, so I don't have to worry about anyone like Madeline and Coco listening in. Gossip is their oxygen.

"I'm sorry, Kat," Jane says, tucking a strand of mousy-brown hair behind her ear. "It's too late to change partners. The answer is no."

In defeat, I look for Halle in the cafeteria. She's at a table in the corner, hunched over a plate of tofu cheddar casserole. I feel my stomach lurch as I watch her eat. The food looks and smells like dog barf.

"You want some of this?" Halle asks. "It's better than it looks."

I tell her I'm not hungry and fill her in on what happened with Jane. Halle puts down her fork. "I can't believe Jane won't switch you," she says. "It's so unfair."

"I know. But she said it's too late to change."

"Even though Sam kissed you?"

"I didn't tell her *that*. Why would I?"

"True," Halle says. "It just sucks—that's all."

Sucks is one way to put it. But you know what sucks worse? Sam's dumb apology texts. He's been sending them all weekend. The latest one came this morning:

> I am SOOOOOO sorry, Kat!
>
> I was way out of line.
>
> Please forgive me.
>
> PLEASE!!!! ☺ ☺ ☺

I'm not sure whether I should accept Sam's apology or not. I can forgive Mom, who genuinely seems sorry and ordered sushi as proof. But Sam? All he's done is send a bunch of shouty texts with smiley-face emojis. If he wants me to forgive him, he'll have to try harder than that.

While I'm thinking this over, I catch Halle scanning the cafeteria for you-know-who. He wasn't in class this morning, and Halle thinks he's sick. "I should text him," she says, digging in her backpack for her phone. "He might need me to bring him his books."

Bring him his books? What is she now, his personal assistant?

Halle puts away her phone. "What are you smirking at? If you have something to say, say it."

"I wasn't smirking," I say, taking a sip of Halle's water. "But I do have something to say."

"Oh, yeah?" Halle is frowning now.

I nod. "I know you really like Michael, Hal, but you've become totally obsessed with him. It's getting old."

"*Old?*" Halle narrows her eyes. "If I didn't know better, I'd say you're jealous."

"Me, jealous of Michael?" I try not to snort. "That's not it. I'm just getting tired of listening to you talk about him all the time."

Halle mashes her lips together. "I'm sorry you feel that way, Kat, but you're being ridiculous. You're just mad that I've got someone who likes me and no one is interested in *you*."

"That's not true," I say, trying to think of boys (other than Sam) who like me. There's Justin, a kid on the fifth floor who says hi in the elevator, and William, Henry's friend from preschool who sits on my lap during playdates, and . . . oh, who cares! "Fine," I say, just to smooth things over. "But I mean it about Michael, Hal. If you like him that much, *tell* him already."

"You said you would do it!"

Oh boy. Not that again. "First, I said no such thing. Second, talking to your crush is your job, not mine."

Halle swats away my comment like a pesky mosquito. "I still say you're jealous. So jealous, you can *taste* it."

I know a losing battle when I see one. "Can we talk about something else?" I say. "Please?"

"Fine." Halle leans back in her seat. "This conversation was starting to bore me anyway."

I ignore her. "Halloween is twenty-two days away and I'm thinking of going as Ms. Frizzle from *The Magic School Bus*."

Halle shrugs. "So?"

"So . . . I'll decorate a blue thrift-store dress with stars and planets, borrow my mom's pointy red shoes, and put up my hair in a messy bun. I might even carry around a stuffed-animal lizard, if I can find one. What about you?"

"I'm not dressing up this year," Halle says. "It's babyish."

I can't believe what I'm hearing. Halle loves Halloween as much as I do. Maybe even more. Last year she started planning her costume in July. She even sent me a three-page letter from camp, outlining the pros and cons of each possible idea. Could her lack of interest in her favorite holiday be a symptom of her crush on Michael? I try not to panic. "You're still going trick-or-treating with me, aren't you? Say yes!"

"Well . . ."

"There'll be candy," I say. "Lots and lots of *candy* . . ."

Halle grins. "You know me too well."

I laugh, relieved things are back on track. Best friends don't have to agree on everything. It's just nice when we do.

20.

Prank Call

On Saturday I go to Halle's for a sleepover. It's nice to have it be just us for a change. No Henry. No babysitting. Just me and Halle.

"Let's prank call Michael!" she says, leaping onto her bed. "Go get your phone."

I look up from the beanbag chair where I'm letting my sparkly purple toenail polish dry. Clearly our conversation at lunch the other day didn't get through to her. Halle is still riding the Michael McGraw crush train. "Why would we want to prank Michael?" I ask, watching Halle bounce up and down on the springy mattress. "And on *my* phone?"

"First, it's fun," Halle says, "and second, he'll know it's

me if we use mine." She points to my overnight bag. "Phone. Go. Get."

I inspect a smudged pinkie toe. "Forget it."

"Then I'll use my own phone."

"No, you won't. It's a bad idea."

Halle stops bouncing. "Come on, Kat. Don't be such a party pooper."

"I'm not," I say. "I just don't think pranking Michael is a good idea. He'll think it's annoying."

"True." Halle flops down on her belly. "I've got a better idea."

"Which is . . . ?"

"I'll pretend I have a question about the Harriet project. We're partners, after all."

"Yeah, but that doesn't mean he'll want to talk about school stuff on a Saturday night."

Halle sits up and bites off a hangnail. "You're right. You should call him."

"*Me?*"

"Yeah. You can talk about random stuff, like how his weekend is going. Then you'll ask what he thinks of me—whether he likes me or not. It's a perfect plan!"

"I don't know," I say. "Wouldn't it be easier to just talk to him yourself?"

"Easy?" Halle heaves a monster sigh. "We've been over this before, Kat. Asking a boy whether he likes you or not is the *opposite* of easy. And nobody does that! Maybe if you'd ever had a crush on someone, you'd know."

At first I'm not sure how to take this. Should I be insulted? Storm out of Halle's room and take my best-friend-sleepover business elsewhere? But Halle's right. I've never had a crush on anyone. At least not one I'm aware of.

"Please, Kat," Halle says. "Just one little call. For me?" She clasps her hands together, begging.

"Okay, fine. But you owe me."

Halle grins as she runs off to get my phone. I watch as she digs it out of my overnight bag and punches in Michael's number. Of course she's got it memorized. "Here," she says, thrusting the phone at me. "It's ringing!"

I put the phone to my ear. "Hello?" I hear loud chewing, followed by a gulp. I wonder what Michael is eating. Beef jerky, maybe? Cheetos?

"Kat!" Michael says. "What's up?"

"Um, not much." I know I'm supposed to ask how his weekend is going, but now it seems stupid. I shoot Halle a help-me look.

"Ask him what he thinks of me," Halle hisses. "Go!"

I clear my throat. "So, Michael. What do you think of Halle?"

"Halle?" Michael takes another bite of whatever he's eating. "I dunno. I never thought about it. But what's the deal with you and Teitelbaum? You like him, or what?"

Huh? Why would Michael think I'm interested in Sam? Ever since he kissed me, I've done my best to pretend Sam doesn't exist. Except when we have to work on the Harriet project. Then I don't have a choice. "Sam?" I finally say. "You can't be serious."

Halle gives me a sharp poke. "Why are you talking about Sam? This is supposed to be about me." I wave her away.

"I didn't mean to, like, insult you or anything," Michael says. "I was just wondering."

"Oh." I hear rustling. More chewing. What is he *eating*?

When he starts talking again, his voice is so quiet, I can barely hear him. "I . . . um, want to tell you something," Michael says.

"Yeah?"

"Well, I, uh . . . I wouldn't want you to, um, like *Teitelbaum* or anything. Because, well . . . I think you're really cool, Kat."

Wait. Is Michael saying what I think he's saying?

"I just wanted you to know that," he says, gaining confidence. "You're a cool Kat." He laughs at his little joke.

"Okay," I say. "Bye!" I drop the phone as if it's about to scald my palm.

"What was that about?" Halle asks. "You look like you've seen a ghost."

"Nothing," I say, slipping the phone in my back pocket. "Want to order a pizza?"

"I want to know what Michael said about me."

I feel my face heating up. "He wasn't very specific," I say. "You know . . . boys."

Halle isn't going for it. "I'm sure he said *something*. Come on, Kat. Tell me."

If Halle's apartment had a fire escape, I'd make like a burglar and sneak out the window—but it doesn't. I try again. "He thinks I like Sam, so I had to hang up. I mean, *gross*." I screw up my face for emphasis.

Halle sits down on the bed. "Why would Michael care if you like Sam?"

"He doesn't," I tell her. "He was just looking for something to say."

"Oh." Halle gives me a funny look, but she doesn't say more. She just gets up and says she'll ask her mom to order us a pizza.

Once she's out of the room, I flop back into the beanbag chair and try not to scream. What just happened? How is it possible that Michael likes me? I thought he liked Halle! Sure, I didn't realize it at first—like at the first rap session, when he said he liked a girl who was "nice, and cool, and funny." He could've been talking about anyone. But later, when he waved at Halle in the hall, and stared at her in the cafeteria while she was eating her grilled cheese, it was obvious. I know because I was right next to her each time!

And then a horrible thought worms its way into my brain. What if the girl Michael was talking about in rap session—and waving to in the hall, and staring at in the cafeteria—wasn't Halle?

What if it was . . . *me*?

21.

Intuition

On Monday morning I find a note taped to my desk. I open it up and start reading:

> Dear Kat,
> Your the best, better then the rest
> When I look at you I want to smile
> Not for a minute but for a while
> Your hair is brown your teeth are white
> I really think your DINOMITE . . .

Oh *no*. Michael McGraw has written me a poem. A love poem, with bad spelling. Thank goodness Halle is at the orthodontist. Otherwise, I'd be planning my own funeral. I stuff the note in my pocket and avoid Michael's moony eyeballs for the rest of homeroom.

Later, in the hall, Halle spies her crush gazing at me from behind the water fountain. "Why is Michael staring at you?"

"He's staring at *you*," I say. "Isn't it obvious?"

"No," Halle says, narrowing her eyes. "It's not."

"Well..."

"What did he say on the phone, Kat? I know there's more than you're telling me."

"It was nothing," I lie. "Just stuff about Sam. I told you already."

"Then tell me again. And don't leave anything out this time. I want to know everything."

I fight the urge to bite my nails. "I don't remember."

Halle makes a face and walks off down the corridor. She doesn't turn around to see if I'm following her.

In carpentry, Halle catches Michael gaping at me while I'm hammering nails into the bookshelf I'm making, and again at lunch, as I'm eating my pasta primavera. By the time we're in PE, finishing up a unit on rhythmic gymnastics, Halle's had enough. The fact that Michael is waving at me from across the room isn't helping.

"What's going on, Kat?" she asks, rolling a wooden hoop for me to jump through. "I know it's something."

I squat down to pick up the fallen hoop. "I have no idea what you're talking about."

Halle glowers at me, hands on hips. "You don't expect me to believe that, do you? It's obvious that—"

Halle doesn't get to finish. Michael is standing right in front of us. "Hey," he says, nodding at me. "Whaddya think of my poem?"

"Poem?" Halle frowns. "What poem?"

"The one I wrote for Kat," Michael says. "Poetry's kinda my thing."

Before I have time to explain, Halle snatches the gymnastics hoop out of my hand and stomps over to Madeline and Coco.

❧

In rap session Halle's hand is the first to go up. "The person I trust most in the world—and I won't name names—is doing something behind my back. Something sneaky."

My best friend doesn't have to name names. All eyes are on me. Madeline's and Coco's glares feel the strongest.

"Are you sure about this, Halle?" Olympia asks. "For all you know, it could be a misunderstanding."

"Oh, it's no misunderstanding," Halle tells her. "I feel it in my gut."

"Maybe you're lactose intolerant," Wilson says, adjusting the cuffs of his lab coat.

"What does that have to do with anything?" Halle asks.

Wilson puts out his hand for the talking stick. "People with sensitive digestive systems have an incredible sense of intuition. I read about it in last month's *New England Journal of Medicine*."

"Wilson's right," Liberty says, taking the stick. "If you think this person is doing something sneaky behind your back and your stomach is acting up, well . . . she probably is."

"How do you know it's a *she*?" Sam says, taking the stick from Liberty. "Halle could be talking about a guy." I shoot Sam a grateful smile. I've been avoiding him all week, but he's still on my side.

"It's not me!" Kevin yells.

"Me neither," Hector says. "I'm not a sneaky person."

"But you're weird," Madeline tells him. "And you think you were abducted by aliens."

"I was," Hector says. "At Yankee Stadium. I was waiting in line for a hot dog, when all of a sudden this little green man hopped out of a spaceship and—"

Olympia holds up her hand. "Do you have the talking stick, Hector?"

Hector looks down at his stick-less hands. "No."

"Then it's not your turn to speak." Olympia takes the stick from Sam and gives it to Halle. "Please continue," she says.

Halle shifts in her seat. "As I was saying, this person—who shall remain nameless—is trying to steal my crush. I never thought she'd do something like that, but obviously I was wrong."

I feel like running out of the room. Why did Halle

have to say *she*? Everyone knows it's me, but she didn't have to be so obvious about it. Why couldn't she have listened when Olympia said this could be a misunderstanding? As Ole Golly tells Harriet: "People are hurt more by misunderstanding than anything else." Can't Halle see this is exactly the same thing?

As I'm about to ask for the talking stick, Michael slaps his hand against his head. "Oh no!"

Olympia's forehead creases in concern. "What's wrong, Michael?"

"I just remembered something."

"Fine, but what did we say about interrupting the speaker?"

"It's rude?"

"And . . ."

"Inconsiderate?"

Olympia nods. "Exactly."

"But can I say one thing?" Michael says. "It's important."

Olympia turns to Halle. "Does Michael have your permission to speak?"

Halle can't hand the stick over fast enough.

Michael jumps to his feet. "The Yankees beat the Red Sox last night—seven-three. Their losing streak is officially OVER!"

"Yes!" Kevin pumps his fist in the air. "Finally!"

"Whew," adds Hector. "I was beginning to give up hope."

Olympia, who usually has the patience of a Buddhist monk, has had enough. "Let's turn our attention back to Halle," she says, putting out her hand for the talking stick. "She's been waiting patiently to continue."

"That's okay," Halle says, gazing at Michael. "I'm done."

I'm dying to reach for the stick and tell the class I'm not the sneaky backstabber Halle says I am, but why bother? Nobody would believe me anyway. When rap session is over, I pick up my backpack and follow my classmates out the door.

"Kat?" It's Olympia, catching up to me in the hall. "Do you have a few minutes to chat?"

This "chat," I'm guessing, is not about Halle. "I, um . . . have to see the nurse," I say. "I think I'm coming down with something."

"Oh, this won't take long." Olympia gestures for me to follow her to her office. "Come on."

Clearly I don't have a choice. I'm going with her.

22.

The Jelly-Bean Chain

The first thing I notice about Olympia's office is that it's messy. Books are scattered everywhere, with stacks of manila folders propped up against the walls and under the bookshelves. Mom would freak if she saw this.

Olympia directs me to a large overstuffed chair next to her desk. The fabric has faded to a powdery blue and is smeared with suspicious stains. I wonder how many other Village Calamity kids have sat in this chair. A lot, I'll bet. Maybe even Mom.

"Make yourself comfy," Olympia says. "And have some jelly beans." She points to a glass jar on her desk. I reach in and fish out three pink ones. When I pop them in my mouth, I taste grapefruit. Not my favorite flavor, but a jelly bean is a jelly bean.

While I'm chewing, I sneak a peek at the bulletin board over Olympia's desk. Every inch is covered with postcards, campaign buttons, and bumper stickers. A picture near the top catches my eye. It's Olympia with President Obama. The photo must have been taken a long time ago, because Olympia's face is less wrinkled and her hair looks different: still orange, but loose and flowing. I wonder why she got to hang out with such a famous person, but it feels nosy to ask.

"Great photo, isn't it?"

I feel my cheeks get hot. "I've never met anyone famous," I admit. "Was it cool?"

"*Really* cool." Olympia smiles at the memory. "I met Mr. Obama before he was elected president, in 2008, at a campaign rally in Washington Square Park. His campaign manager's cousin was married to my college roommate, so I was allowed backstage."

"Wow."

"I was nervous to meet him," Olympia adds, "but he was very gracious and down to earth. It was quite an experience." She kicks off her Birkenstocks and pretzels her legs underneath her. "You're probably wondering why I asked to see you, Kat."

Well, now that you mention it . . .

"I wanted to talk to you about our last email exchange."

Oh *no*. I never wrote back, I realize. It's not that I didn't want to. I just didn't know what to say. I still don't, even now that I'm sitting here, watching Olympia watching me. As much as I want to share my feelings, I don't know where to start. There's so much.

"You're having a tough time with your mom," Olympia prompts. "Right?"

I lift my eyes from the floor.

"You can trust me, Kat. I won't say anything, to anyone. Not even your mom, unless you want me to."

"I don't," I say quickly. "I'd rather keep this . . ." I search for the right words. "Just between us." I pause. "Can I have a glass of water?"

"You got it." Olympia goes over to a small refrigerator in the corner of the room and takes out a jug of water. She finds a glass, fills it, and hands it to me.

While I'm drinking, Olympia takes a handful of jelly beans from the jar and lays them out on her desk, bean to bean. A jelly-bean chain. She stares at it thoughtfully before motioning for me to put down my empty glass. "So, let's try something," she says. "Each jelly bean represents a thought. You'll take a jelly bean from the top, eat it, and then say the first thing that pops into your mind. You won't overthink your statement, and you won't pass judgment on it. You'll just talk. Then you'll move on to the next jelly bean. Sound okay?"

I nod. Although Olympia's idea seems a bit strange, I reach for the green jelly bean at the top of the chain and pop it in my mouth. When I'm done scraping the last sugary bits off with my tongue, I look over at

Olympia. "My mom has OCD," I say. "At least I think she does."

I expect to feel ashamed for saying this out loud, for using the medical term I'd Googled. But shame is the last thing I'm feeling. It's relief. Relief that I'm finally able to take the lid off the dirty-laundry hamper—even if it's just a crack.

"Go on," Olympia says. "You feel . . ."

"Scared."

"Scared of . . . ?"

I know I'm not supposed to overthink my feelings, or judge them. I'm supposed tell Olympia the truth, the whole truth, and nothing but the truth. But the truth feels impossible to say out loud. I mean, how can I tell Olympia that I find Mom's problem, her OCD, difficult to understand and I'm scared I might get it too? And how can I admit that I haven't talked to my dad about this? Olympia will ask. And when she does . . . ? I don't know what to tell her. It's like when I was little and couldn't jump in the deep end of the pool. I wanted to, but I always chickened out at the last minute. This pool is deeper, though—and way scarier.

"I need to go," I say, reaching for my backpack.

"That's fine, Kat, but—"

Before Olympia can finish her sentence, I'm out the door.

23.

It's Your Honesty That's Hostile

After school I find Mom in the bathroom, spritzing the bathtub with spray bleach. Her phone is on the counter, displaying the timer function. This is odd. If Mom's not going on *Clean Sweep*, why is she using a timer? Could this be a new symptom of her OCD? And if it is, how do I make it go away?

Mom puts down the spray bottle when she sees me. "Guess what?"

"What?"

"I've changed my mind about *Clean Sweep*. I'm doing it."

"You are?"

Mom smiles. "The taping is a week from Friday. You

can bring a friend if you'd like. Your dad and Barbara will be there too."

I feel as if the air has been sucked out of the room. Mom's changed her mind? And she invited *Dad*? How is this possible? Mom never changes her mind, and she only talks to Dad when she has to. As Ole Golly says to Harriet: "Life is very strange." I plop down on the toilet lid. "What made you change your mind?" I ask.

Mom peels off her rubber gloves and sits down on the edge of the tub. "For starters, there's no sense worrying about what's to come after the show. I might not even win."

"Right . . ." I say.

"But that's not the main reason," Mom admits. Her eyes find mine. "I did a lot of thinking after our fight, Kit-Kat. About what happened between us, and my behavior in general."

I sit up straighter. Is Mom about to admit she has OCD? Or is there something else she wants to tell me? I hold my breath, waiting.

"I know I haven't been making life easy for you lately," Mom says. "With all the cleaning and stuff."

"You're not doing it on purpose," I tell her. "You can't help it."

"I know, but still." Mom looks down at her hands. "I need to make some changes around here, Kat. Big ones. *Clean Sweep* is just one of them."

"What do you mean?" I ask.

"Well . . ." Mom adjusts her bandanna. "I know my cleaning is a problem. The hand-washing too. I'm hoping that doing the show might turn things around for me. You know, put myself out there . . . channel my problem into something good."

What Mom's saying kind of makes sense, even if it doesn't 100 percent explain why she changed her mind. Still, I'm proud of her for trying. And for being honest with me. It's a big step.

Just as I'm leaning over to give her a hug, I feel my phone vibrate in my back pocket. I take it out to see who's calling. It's Sam. In all the drama with Halle— and now, with Mom changing her mind about *Clean Sweep*—I had forgotten we'd planned a "conference call" (Sam's words) to discuss the Harriet project. "Sorry, Mom," I say, jumping to my feet. "I have to take this." I run into my room and sit down on the bed.

"I think we should mention that The Boy with the Purple Socks isn't the kid's real name," Sam says right away. "It's Peter. Peter Matthews."

"Well, duh," I say. "Everybody knows that."

"It was only a suggestion, Kat. You don't have to be hostile."

"I wasn't being hostile. Just honest."

"Then it's your honesty that's hostile. If I didn't know better, I'd say you're still mad."

I want to say something snarky like, "Good guess, Einstein," or better yet, hang up. But I don't want Sam to tell Jane I'm difficult to work with. "Can we get back to the project now?" I say. "Please?"

"Okay, fine." Sam tries again. "How about the fact that Pinky Whitehead is so pale and thin, he looks like a glass of milk?"

"That's a description of what Pinky Whitehead *looks* like, Sam. It's not important. What's wrong with you?"

"What's wrong with *you?*"

"Nothing. I'm trying to do well on the Harriet project, and you're coming up with silly ideas."

Sam doesn't answer at first. Finally he says, "I think we should talk some other time, Kat. You know, before one of us says something mean."

Like Halle, Sam's got it all wrong. I'm not mean. I'm just upset that my friends are turning against me: Sam by trying to kiss me, and Halle by thinking I'm a sneaky backstabber. Unfortunately I don't get a chance to tell Sam how I feel. He's hung up on me.

I stare at my phone in disbelief. Sam, hanging up on *me?* I didn't know he had it in him. And then the ringer goes off again. Sam calling to apologize, I assume. I knew he couldn't stay mad for long. But it's not Sam's voice I hear when I answer. It's deeper, with loud music in the background.

"We didn't get to finish talking on Saturday night," Michael says into the phone. "I was telling you I like you, but you hung up."

"Um, I . . ."

"So, here's the deal," Michael continues. "I think you're cool, and I know you like me too. So we should, you know, hang out or something."

"Hang out?" I grip the phone tighter. "I don't think—"

"Cool. I'll text you my schedule. Check you later, Kat."

"You don't need to—"

The line goes dead.

Which is what I'll be when Halle finds out that her crush called to say I'm cool and that he'll text me his schedule.

D-e-a-d.

24.

Myself Again

When my alarm rings the next morning, I feel like throwing it out the window. The thought of going to school, where Halle thinks I'm a backstabbing crush stealer and Michael might leave me another dopey love poem, makes my stomach hurt. I'm also feeling bad about being mean(ish) to Sam and bailing on Olympia. Maybe I shouldn't have been so hard on Sam. And maybe Olympia was only trying to help me—but I wouldn't let her. I roll out of bed and get my computer.

TO: Olympia.Rabinowitz@VillageHumanity.org
SUBJECT: I'm sorry
DATE: October 17 7:05:42 AM EDT
FROM: Kat.Greene@VillageHumanity.org

Dear Olympia,

I'm sorry I ran out of your office yesterday. Talking about problems is harder than writing about them, I guess. I hope you're not mad.

Oh and guess what? My mom changed her mind about *Clean Sweep*. She's doing it. The taping is a week from Friday. I'll let you know how it turns out. She thinks this will make everything better. I hope so. I also hope she wins the money.

I consider telling Olympia about the situation with Halle, but I don't. With any luck, things will be back to normal by the time I get to school. I sign my name and send the email.

❧

Halle ignores me when I walk into the classroom, and later, in carpentry, she refuses to pass me the nails. By lunchtime, she's still not talking to me. "This has got to stop," I say, plunking down with my cafeteria tray. "I'm not interested in Michael, Hal—I swear. You've got to believe me. We're best friends!"

Halle takes an angry bite of her free-range chicken leg. "That's what I thought, until you tried to steal him away from me."

I could argue, but I know it won't help. Instead, I tell her about Mom's last-minute decision to go on *Clean Sweep*. "The taping's next Friday and I can bring a friend.

We'll miss school and everything. My mom already checked."

Halle throws down her chicken leg. "If you think I'm going anywhere with you, you're nuts! And that includes trick-or-treating on Halloween. You can go with Michael, for all I care."

I feel as if I've been kicked in the stomach. I thought for sure Halle would say yes to *Clean Sweep*. Missing school for a TV show taping is like Christmas and your birthday all rolled up in one. And not going trick-or-treating together? Impossible. "You don't mean it," I say, reaching for my best friend's arm. "You're just mad."

"Oh, I mean it, all right."

Just then Michael appears at our table. A strip of beef jerky dangles from the side of his mouth like a gangster's cigar. "Thought I'd come over and say hi," he tells us.

Halle's eyes narrow. "To me or to her?"

Michael puts down his tray. "Can't I say hi to both of you?"

"You can," Halle says. "But I wouldn't recommend it."

"Why not?" Michael says.

"Come on, Hal," I say under my breath. "You don't need to do this. It's stupid."

"Oh yeah?" Before I can stop her, Halle is heading to the other end of the table, where Madeline and Coco are daintily picking at salads. I watch as she sits down and joins the girls' conversation.

"Now look what you've done," I say to Michael. "She hates me more than ever."

"Why would she hate you?" Michael says.

"It's a long story," I say.

"I like stories," Michael says, snatching a sweet-potato fry off my plate. "And I like you."

"I like you too, Michael. But I don't *like*-like you—not the way Halle does. Or haven't you noticed?"

"Noticed what?"

"That Halle likes you. She talks about you all the time."

"She does?" Michael cranes his neck for a better view of Halle at the other end of the table.

"Yeah," I say. "A *lot*."

"Well, I dunno . . ." Michael takes off his Yankees cap and scratches his head. I've never seen him at a loss for words before, but there's a first time for everything. "Do you think I should talk to her?" he asks.

"Why not?" I say. "Halle would probably—"

But I'm talking to myself. Michael has picked up his tray and is squeezing in next to Halle.

Well, that was quick.

I scan the lunchroom for someone to eat with, ruling out Halle and Michael immediately. Madeline and Coco too. Wilson is examining Liberty's nose piercing with a flashlight, and Kevin and Hector are shooting spitballs at the fourth graders.

That leaves Sam.

The problem is, I'm supposed to be mad at Sam. But staying mad at Sam is harder than it looks. He stuck up for me in rap session, and he cares about getting good grades—which I really do admire. Now, watching him eat his pasta alone, I kind of feel sorry for him. I get up with my tray.

"Kat!" Sam's face lights up like a glow stick. "To what do I owe this pleasure?"

"I want to make up," I say, taking a seat across from him. He's got a smear of tomato sauce on his chin, but I don't mention it. I'm here to apologize, not criticize his table manners. "You did something wrong, but I'm tired of being mad at you."

"That's nice of you, Kat," Sam says. "I really am sorry."

"I know you are."

"And I'm sorry for hanging up on you yesterday. I shouldn't have done that."

"I kind of deserved it," I admit.

"Does that mean we're friends again?"

"Yeah, under one condition."

"Anything." Sam blinks at me behind his glasses.

"You'll come with me to see my mom compete on *Clean Sweep*. It's a TV game show, and the taping's a week from Friday." Now that Halle hates me, Sam's the closest thing I have to a best friend.

Sam sticks out his hand for me to shake. "Deal."

I take his hand and shake back. And for the first time in ages—since my fight with Mom and since Halle started ignoring me—I feel like myself again. Somewhere between jump-for-joy happy and down-in-the-dumps sad. It's not ideal, but I can live with it. For now.

25.

Showtime

On the morning of the *Clean Sweep* taping, Mom speed-cleans the kitchen one last time before changing out of her overalls. We eat a quick breakfast and then take a cab to the studio in Midtown. Sam and his mother are waiting for us in the lobby.

"Good luck, Deidre," Mrs. Teitelbaum says, pecking Mom on the cheek. "We're all rooting for you." Sam's mom looks exactly like Sam, with curly auburn hair and a sprinkling of freckles across the bridge of her nose. If she weren't wearing a dress, she and Sam could be twins. Mrs. Teitelbaum hugs Mom good-bye and scurries off to work, leaving the three of us to wait for further instructions.

"I'm really nervous," Mom says, chewing her lip. "What if I lose?"

"You won't lose," I tell her. "No way."

"Kat's right, Mrs. G.," Sam says, patting Mom on the back like a gassy baby. "You've got this in the bag."

"Well, I have been practicing," Mom says.

"Practicing" is an understatement. The timer has barely left Mom's hand since she changed her mind about the show. If she doesn't win, it's not because she didn't try hard enough.

As Sam and I take turns building Mom's confidence, a skinny guy with a clipboard appears to take Mom to the wardrobe department. "Ready, Deidre?" he asks.

Mom turns to me and Sam. "I'd better go," she says. "Wish me good luck."

"Good luck, Mom," I say, giving her a squeeze.

"Break a leg, Mrs. G.," Sam tells her. "You'll be great!"

Mom gives us a shaky smile and follows the guy down the hall. I turn to Sam. "What if she doesn't win? She'll be so disappointed."

"Relax," Sam says, motioning for me to follow him into the auditorium. "Your mom's been practicing. She said so herself."

"I know, but . . ." I trail Sam to the third row, where Dad and Barbara are already seated. Thank goodness they had the sense to leave Henry home with the babysitter.

As I take my seat, the overhead lights dim and a

stocky guy in a tight black T-shirt makes his way onto the brightly lit set. The neon CLEAN SWEEP sign is blinking on and off behind him like a billboard in Times Square. I don't spot any of the dirty kitchen appliances yet, but I do notice an assortment of cleaning products lined up in neat, even rows along the back wall. I'll bet Mom can't wait to get her hands on them.

"I'm Tommy Z.," the announcer tells the crowd, "and I'm here to explain the rules for audience participation."

"Hi, Tommy!" a blond lady calls out. She's wearing an I ♥ NY sweatshirt and fanning herself with a tourist map.

Tommy Z. walks closer to the audience and continues his instructions. "So, when the applause sign is on, you're going to . . ."

"Clap!" Sweatshirt Lady yells from her seat.

"That's right," Tommy Z. says, smiling patiently at her. If he finds her annoying, he doesn't let on. "How loud?"

"Really loud!"

"And if the applause sign *isn't* on?"

"We should be quiet!" Sweatshirt Lady puts a finger up to her lips.

"Right again! I can tell you've done this before."

While Sweatshirt Lady is giggling behind her hand at Tommy Z.'s comment, I catch a glimpse of the Sweepers offstage. Mom is biting her nails and looks as green as her sanitation worker's uniform. I nudge Sam with my elbow. "My mom looks nervous."

"She'll be fine, Kat. Don't worry." I want to believe him, but how can I? There's so much at stake—for Mom, and for me.

"Now, without further ado," Tommy Z. says, "please put your hands together for the host of our show, the one, the only . . . Mr. Bing Monroe!"

The crowd starts clapping like crazy when Bing Monroe strides onto the stage, carrying a broom. "Welcome to *Clean Sweep*, folks!" he says. "The show where a little elbow grease can make one lucky winner very, very rich!" The applause sign isn't on, but people are hooting and hollering and stomping their feet. Some are taking pictures, even though it's probably not allowed.

While I'm taking this all in, Mom marches across the stage with the other Sweepers. She's not biting her nails, but her face is still green.

"Don't worry," Sam says, reading my mind. "Your mom will be fine."

Maybe Sam's right, but I don't say anything back. I'm too focused on Mom and on Bing Monroe, who's now introducing today's five lucky contestants.

"And last but not least," Bing is saying, "we have Deidre Greene, a stay-at-home mom from right here in the Big Apple." Bing winks and steps closer to Mom. "I hear you're quite the cleaning pro, Dee. What's your favorite product?"

Mom fiddles with the reflective strip on her orange safety vest. "Well, I like Windex for removing fingerprints on glass surfaces, and I . . . I . . . like Pine-Sol for, um . . ."

I lean across Sam so I can whisper to Dad. "Does Mom look strange to you?"

"She's dressed like a sanitation worker and carrying a broom, honey. Of course she looks strange."

"That's not what I mean, Dad. I think there's something wrong with her."

Sam adjusts his glasses. "I think Kat's right, Mr. Greene."

Now I'm worried. So worried, that when Bing Monroe asks Mom whether she's ready to sweep off with the big money, my heart does jumping jacks in my chest.

"So, are you, Deidre?" Bing Monroe asks again, only louder this time. "Ready to sweep off with twenty-five thousand dollars in cash and a lifetime supply of cleaning products?"

Mom isn't listening. She's staring at the camera like a hunted animal.

"Deidre?" Bing Monroe waves his hand in front of her face. "Earth to Deidre? Come in, Deidre . . ." He's chuckling into the microphone, but his eyes aren't laughing. They're fixed on the cameraman offstage.

"Sam," I say, clutching my friend's arm, "I'm scared."

"Your mom's just nervous, Kat. Bing will get her to relax. Watch."

I'd rather not, but I keep my eyes on Mom. She's wriggled out of Bing's grasp and is making her way offstage.

"Deidre," Bing calls after her. "Deidre!"

I watch in horror as Mom staggers across the set and crashes into a barbecue grill. Her legs buckle under her, and she falls to the floor. I hear a scream ring out across the auditorium.

It takes a minute before I realize it's mine.

26.

Torn

"She fainted, sweetheart. It's a common reaction when someone's nervous." Dad is trying to make me feel better as we wait in a small conference room for news about Mom, but it's not working. My armpits are clammy and my legs feel like Jell-O.

"He's right, Kat," Sam says, taking my hand. "Your mom will be fine."

"Absolutely!" Barbara gets up from the conference table and puts her arm around my shoulders. "The excitement of it all probably got to her. She'll be back on her feet in no time, honey. You'll see."

I want to believe Dad, and Sam, and Barbara: that Mom passed out because she was nervous and she'll be back on her feet in no time. But I'm still buzzing with nerves when the studio's doctor walks in with Mom on his arm. She's walking slowly and her face is pale. "Mom!" I run over and throw my arms around her. "Are you okay?"

"Careful," the doctor says. "Your mom's still a bit wobbly."

"Does she need to go to the hospital?" I ask, backing away.

"No, nothing like that. Just bed rest and plenty of fluids. She was probably dehydrated. It's a common cause of fainting, you know."

"That's what my dad said."

The doctor smiles. "You've got a smart dad."

I try to find comfort in the nice doctor's words, but my stomach is churning as Dad and Barbara help Mom out of the building and into a cab. Barbara, Sam, and I climb into the back seat with Mom while Dad sits up front with the driver. By the time we've reached Thirteenth Street, Mom is asleep on Sam's shoulder.

"Easy does it," Dad says, helping Mom to her feet. She shoots him a grateful smile and lets Barbara lead her into our building. I wait outside with Sam while Dad pays the driver.

"I'd better go," I tell Sam when I see Dad coming toward us. "You know . . ."

"Don't worry," Sam says. "Your mom will be fine."

"You think so?"

"I *know* so."

I wish I were so sure. I tell Sam I'll text him later and head upstairs with Dad.

Barbara is in the kitchen making coffee when Dad and I walk in. Mom is on the couch, her arm flung over her eyes. "How are you feeling, Mom?" I ask, plopping down beside her. "Any better?"

"A little," Mom says, trying to sit up.

"Stay where you are," Dad tells her. "You're still weak."

Mom rolls her eyes. "If only you were this attentive when we were married." It's the first joke she's made all day. At least I think it's a joke.

After Barbara joins us in the living room, Dad offers to stay overnight at our place. "I'd like to keep an eye on Kat," he tells Mom. "And on you too."

"I agree," Barbara says. "Let Dennis help you, Dee."

Mom won't hear of it. "That's sweet of you guys, but I don't need a babysitter. I'm fine. Now, if you don't mind, I'm going to my room to lie down."

I watch as Mom moves unsteadily down the hall. When she's gone, Dad turns to me. "Are you sure you don't want me to stay, Kit-Kat? I feel funny leaving you and your mom alone."

"We're not alone," I say. "We have each other."

"I know, but . . ." Dad looks as torn as I feel. I don't want him to leave, but staying overnight would make the situation more awkward than it already is.

"You can go after dinner," I say. "I'll call you before I go to sleep."

"Are you bargaining with me?" Dad smiles slightly. I can tell he's relieved.

"Maybe," I say. For all I know, things will look better tomorrow.

Unfortunately they don't. When I go into the kitchen the next morning, Mom isn't there. She's not in the living room, or in the bathroom either. I head for her bedroom and see the door is shut. I knock. "Mom?"

Nothing.

I knock louder. "Mom?"

Still nothing.

I turn the knob and go in. "Mom . . . ?"

The blinds are closed, but I can make out a small lump in the middle of the bed: Mom, fast asleep. This is strange. Mom never sleeps late, even on weekends. She's usually scrubbing, or polishing, or sterilizing something. I lean over and give her a little shake. "Mom?"

Slowly she opens her eyes. "What time is it?" Her voice sounds like Mrs. Donovan's, our neighbor in 3B who's always smoking outside our building.

"It's almost ten," I say. "You slept for fourteen hours."

Mom doesn't answer. She pulls the blanket over her head and turns to the other side. Suddenly I feel hot all over. Should I be worried? Should I call Dad? But that's dumb. If I know Mom, she'll be back to her old self in no time. I go to my room and wait.

Later, when I'm heating up a can of tomato soup for

Mom's lunch, the phone rings. It's Dad, calling to see how things are going. We chat for a few minutes before he asks to speak to Mom. When I say she's in the shower, the lie sticks to my tongue like peanut butter. I want to tell Dad the truth, but how can I? He'll drag me off to his place for sure. Mom needs me here. I promise to call him later and go back to heating up Mom's soup.

I bring it in to her on a tray. "At least have a bite," I say, handing her a spoon. "It's good."

But Mom doesn't want soup—or anything else. She just wants to sleep.

I try again at two o'clock, and then at four. When Dad calls at dinnertime to see how things are going, I tell him that Mom went to the deli for sandwiches. At nine, when he tries her cell phone, I say she ran down for the mail. "I'm glad she's feeling better," he says, "but have her call me, okay?"

I feel bad lying to Dad, but I don't have a choice. If I tell him that Mom won't eat or get out of bed, I know exactly what will happen. The same goes for writing to Olympia. She'll think Mom's lost it and will get my dad involved. And Halle? She'll only be pity-nice to me, if she talks to me at all.

Scared and out of ideas, I go to bed with a knot in my stomach for the second night in a row. Maybe Mom will be okay tomorrow. She has to be.

27.

Secrets

Mom is still in bed when I go in to check on her the next morning. I've made French toast, which I know she can't resist. Fresh-squeezed orange juice too. "Time to get up," I say, placing the tray on Mom's bed. "Rise and shine!" I go over to the window and open the blinds.

Mom squints at the sunlight streaming through the slats. "Later, Kit-Kat. I'm not hungry."

"Come on, Mom. You've got to have something." I hand her the juice.

Mom pushes it away. "Later," she says again. "Please close the blinds."

"Mom, I don't think—"

"Close them, Kat."

I do as Mom says, but I leave the juice and French toast on her nightstand.

I'm carrying the tray back to the kitchen when I hear my phone ring. I run to my room to get it. It's Dad. But this time, I can't tell more lies. I burst into tears.

"Take a deep breath," Dad tells me. "In through the nose, out through the mouth. Breathe. Breathe. . . ."

In between sobby gulps, I tell Dad what's happening.

"I'll be right there," he says.

I go back to Mom's room and sit on the edge of her bed. I take her hand in mine. Her fingers are redder than ever, and rough as a cat's tongue. When I was little, I never gave her hands much thought. Not when she rubbed my back at bedtime, or braided my hair before school. Or when she put bubbles in my bath, or tied my sneakers at the playground. She was a regular mom who took me to the library for story time and to my friends' houses for playdates and birthday parties. Dad did that stuff too, but it was Mom who knew which books I liked and how to wrap presents with fancy paper and ribbon. Back then, she didn't take her cleaning so . . . *seriously*.

I give Mom's hand a kiss and put it up to my cheek. I keep it there until the doorbell rings. Then I'm out like a flash. I unbolt the door and go boneless in Dad's arms. The tiny buttons on his shirt poke against my face, but I don't care. It feels good to have him here, holding me tight.

Dad untangles himself and drops his jacket on a chair. "Where's your mother?"

I lead him to the bedroom where Mom is still sleeping. We stand over the bed, watching her chest rise and fall as she breathes. After a few minutes Dad motions for me to follow him to the kitchen. He grabs two cans of raspberry seltzer from the refrigerator and sits down at the breakfast bar. He points to the stool next to him. "Sit," he says.

I sit. Then I do what I should have done, long before now.

I tell Dad the whole truth.

I tell him how Mom cleans the apartment, day after day—and how she washes her hands until her fingers are raw. How she embarrasses me by wiping down cans at the supermarket, in her stupid overalls and that red bandanna. How she wears latex gloves, and makes me wear them too.

I tell him how she packed up her wedding china to give to charity, and how she wanted to trash my flea-market rug. How she almost knocked me over in a Snapple-cap tug-of-war, but later apologized and promised to change. And how I worry she never will.

The biggest worry of all, I tell him? That Mom's behavior will only get worse. Which scares me more than anything else. More than keeping secrets, even.

So now Dad knows.

Finally.

I pick up my seltzer and take a big gulp. Dad watches me, frowning. "Why didn't you tell me sooner, sweetheart? I would've done something to help."

"Like what?" I say, choking on the seltzer fizz. "Hide Mom's vacuum cleaner? Take away her rubber gloves?"

"That's not funny, Kat."

"I'm not trying to be," I say. Dad is blaming me for not telling him sooner, but it's not my fault he didn't know. All he had to do was ask. Or even better, open his eyes and *look*.

Dad takes my hand. "Your mom's had a thing about germs for as long as I've known her, Kit-Kat. It wasn't this serious, and it never took over her life the way you're describing now." He pauses. "I tried talking to her about it—many times—but she always said the same thing: that I was making a mountain out of a molehill. After a while it was easier to believe her."

I know what Dad means. Mom said I was making a fuss over nothing too. "Does that mean she has OCD?" I ask, naming Mom's problem for the first time to someone other than Olympia.

Dad nods slowly. "Yeah. I'm pretty sure it does."

We sit with this information for a minute, neither one of us saying anything. Finally Dad puts his arm around me. "I wish I could've done more to help you and your mom, honey. I really am sorry."

I lean in for a hug. "That's okay, Dad. You can help us now."

"I will," he says. "Promise."

I hope it's a promise he can keep.

*

Dad doesn't go home that night. He sleeps on the sofa, getting up every few hours to check in on Mom. I can hear him bumping around in the dark, trying to find his way around the once-familiar apartment. He's still there the next morning when I wander into the kitchen. "Why didn't you wake me?" I ask, glancing at the wall clock. "I'm late for school."

"You're not going to school today," Dad tells me. He pours coffee into a mug and sits down at the breakfast bar.

"But it's Monday," I say, grabbing a muffin from the box on the counter. "I already missed a day for *Clean Sweep*."

After Dad promises I won't get in trouble, he tells me to sit down. I don't have to be psychic to know when bad news is coming. "I want you to come stay with Barbara and me," he says, taking a sip of his coffee. "At least until your mom gets back on her feet."

I feel my throat tighten. "I can't leave Mom. She needs me."

"She needs to get better, Kit-Kat. And she needs to do it alone."

"What do you mean?"

Dad puts down his mug. "Your mom and I talked earlier this morning. She admitted that her problem—

her OCD—is getting worse, and she agreed to seek therapy."

"Oh." I'm glad Mom wants to get help, and I'll bet Olympia will be almost as happy as I am. But I don't understand why I have to move in with Dad. Unless, of course, Mom is going to a mental hospital like Beth Ellen Hansen's mother in *Harriet the Spy*. But Beth Ellen's mother wasn't *really* in a mental hospital. She was "at Biarritz," a ski resort in Switzerland. Does that mean Mom won't be going to one either? I decide to find out anyway—just to be on the safe side.

"Will Mom have to go to a mental hospital?" I ask.

Dad seems surprised by my question. "What would give you that idea?"

"Just something I read," I say. "I know it's silly."

"There's no such thing as a silly question," Dad says. "But no, your mom is not going to a mental hospital. She'll receive outpatient treatment, right here in New York. It's a six-week program, five days a week. Some weekends too."

"Could I stay home with Mom, then?"

"No," Dad says, smiling slightly. "But it wasn't silly to ask."

28.

Welcome to the Jungle

I knew I'd cry when I left for Dad's. I thought Mom would too. But she holds it together as she rolls my blue suitcase into the hall. "This will be hard for both of us, Kit-Kat, but it's for the best."

"How can you be so sure?" I say, folding my arms over my chest.

"I can't," Mom says. She reaches over to tuck a fly-away behind my ear. "But continuing to live like this isn't healthy—for either of us." Mom holds up her hands, which are as raw and cracked as ever. "I have a real problem, Kat, and I need to get help for it. We both know it's time."

Mom is right, but her words sting anyway.

I hold back my tears until I'm outside with Dad,

waiting for a taxi. I expect him to say, "I know this is tough for you, honey," or "Things will get better—wait and see." But he doesn't. He just hands me a tissue and gives me a hug. He doesn't say much during the ride uptown either, or when we're in the elevator going up to his apartment. He must know there aren't words for what I'm feeling.

Barbara and Henry are waiting for us at the front door under a big sign that says, WELCOME, KAT! The bright, slopey letters are Henry's writing, obviously, with some help from Barbara.

"Kitty-Kat!" It's Henry, hopping up and down like a baby kangaroo. "You're here!"

"Hey, bud." I take my suitcase from Dad and follow Barbara into the room I'll be sharing with Henry. The trundle bed has been set up for me, along with a blue-and-white-striped comforter and a set of matching towels. "I hope this is okay," Barbara says, patting the bed. "I know you like blue."

"I like blue!" Henry yells, running in to join us. "And green, and pink, and orange, and purple, and red, and—"

"Why don't we let your sister settle in?" Barbara says, placing her hand on Henry's head. "I'm sure she'd like to unpack." I mouth a quick thank-you to Barbara as she steers Henry out of the room. Then I go for my suitcase.

I've packed some clothes, books for school, and Quackles, a stuffed duck I've had since preschool. I would've brought my Snapple-cap collection, but Halle has it. If she doesn't give it back, I might need to sneak into her room and get it.

I put my clothes in the drawers Barbara cleared out for me and take out my laptop. While I'm getting lost in a cute kitty video, it occurs to me that I should tell Olympia what's going on. She'll find out sooner or later. It might as well come from me.

TO: Olympia.Rabinowitz@VillageHumanity.org
SUBJECT: Trouble
DATE: October 30 2:27:08 PM EDT
FROM: Kat.Greene@VillageHumanity.org

Dear Olympia,

I have a lot to tell you. You know my mom decided to go on *Clean Sweep*, but it didn't turn out the way I hoped. She fainted at the taping and had to be looked at by a doctor. We waited around the studio for a couple of hours and then brought her home. She wouldn't leave her room for the rest of the day or the day after that. It was scary.

Now I'm living with Dad while Mom gets therapy for her OCD. She finally admitted she has it. She'll be going to an outpatient center (Dad explained it to me), which starts tomorrow and ends sometime before Christmas. I don't understand why I can't stay home with Mom, but Dad says she needs space to get

better. Besides, I don't get a choice. I don't get to walk
to school by myself either. Dad's apartment is miles
away from Village Humanity, so he will bring me and
Barbara will pick me up. Sorry to sound so negative,
but life kind of stinks right now.
Kat

A response from Olympia lands in my inbox minutes later.

TO: Kat.Greene@VillageHumanity.org
SUBJECT: Re: Trouble
DATE: October 30 2:34:29 PM EDT
FROM: Olympia.Rabinowitz@VillageHumanity.org

Dear Kat,
     I'm so sorry to hear about your mom. The situation
at the TV studio—and later, at home—must have been
very scary for you. I'm glad your mom is getting help,
though, and that your dad is being supportive. My
thoughts and good wishes are with her—and with you.
Would you like to meet in my office tomorrow to talk
about any of this? I'll be in early.
My best,
Olympia

I don't need to think twice before typing out my
answer.

TO: Olympia.Rabinowitz@VillageHumanity.org
SUBJECT: Re: re: Trouble
DATE: October 30 3:09:32 PM EDT
FROM: Kat.Greene@VillageHumanity.org

Dear Olympia,

    I'll be there. Thanks.

Kat

яе

Barbara orders sushi for dinner and asks me to set the table. I know she's trying to distract me with my favorite food, but I can't forget why I'm here. Everything I see, or think, or feel, or do, reminds me of Mom—and that I can't go home until she's better.

I shouldn't complain, though. It's okay at Dad's. I have my own bed, enough space for my stuff, and Dad and Barbara have been going out of their way to make me feel welcome. But Dad's home is not *home*-home, no matter how hard he and Barbara try.

Henry's wails interrupt my thoughts. "I'm not eating that! It's *waw*!" He points at an eel-and-avocado roll and screws up his face. "Yucky!"

"The eel isn't raw *or* yucky," Dad says, spearing a piece of the roll with his chopsticks. "It's cooked. You'll like it, Henry. Try a bite."

"Yeah, Hen," I say, sitting down next to him. "It's good."

Henry shakes his head from side to side. "No!"

Without a word, Barbara gets up from the table and returns with a bowl of pasta. She places it in front of Henry and hands him a fork. My brother's eyes light up at the sight of familiar food. I watch as he digs in, noodles flying out of his mouth and landing in his lap. He gets some on the floor too. Barbara turns to me with a smile. "Welcome to the jungle," she says.

After we're done eating and Henry's run off to the family room to watch TV, Dad gets up to clear the table. "Is your costume ready?" he asks, gathering the empty sushi containers. "I know mine is."

Oh *no*. Halloween! With everything that's been happening, I'd forgotten it's tomorrow. I tell Dad I'm not going.

"You can't skip Halloween," he says, fumbling with the boxes he's holding. "It's your favorite holiday!"

"It's *your* favorite holiday, Dad."

Barbara laughs as she helps Dad clean up. "I think Kat should do what she wants, Dennis. If she's not up to going, don't push her."

"I wasn't pushing," Dad says. "Just encouraging."

"Well, stop encouraging, then. Right, Kat?"

"Right," I tell Barbara. "I don't mind missing it this year. Seriously. I'll hand out candy."

"Well, *I'm* not missing it," Dad says, heading for the family room to put Henry to bed. "I'm going as Sandy from *Grease!*"

I can't help but giggle.

29.

Strong

The jelly beans are already lined up on Olympia's desk when I walk into her office the next morning. "Welcome," Olympia says, smiling up at me. I'm relieved to see she's not wearing a Halloween costume. I don't think I could take our meeting seriously if she was dressed like Darth Vader or something.

I plop down in the blue easy chair and give Olympia a quick update on how Mom's doing. Then I choose my first bean: marshmallow. "I don't get why my mom likes to clean so much," I say, popping the jelly bean in my mouth. "Cleaning's not fun."

"True," Olympia says, adjusting a silver bangle. "But your mom doesn't clean because she enjoys it, Kat. It's a compulsion. A symptom of her OCD."

Thanks to my Google search, I know what a compulsion is. It's when your brain tells you to do something, whether you want to do it or not. The thing is, I'm not sure how this relates to Mom. I ask Olympia to explain to it me.

"Of course." Olympia leans forward on her elbows. "A person with OCD is bombarded with unwanted thoughts. To stop these thoughts, certain routines, or 'rituals,' must be performed, like double-checking the locks, repeating certain words, tapping, washing your hands—"

"My mom does that," I say. "When she's not cleaning, that is."

"That must be hard to live with," Olympia says. "And tough to watch."

"I guess," I say.

Olympia eyes me carefully. "Your mom's rituals affect you too, you know. Even if it's only indirectly."

"Yeah, well . . ." I look at the clock opposite the bookshelf. "I probably shouldn't miss all of homeroom," I say, getting up from the chair, "so thanks for—"

"Please sit down, Kat." Olympia steps away from her desk and plops down on the floor in front of me. She crisscrosses her legs like a yogi. "Talking about feelings isn't easy, but we should try to continue for a bit. Remember, you've been bottling up stuff for quite some time and now you're dealing with the consequences. You have every right to feel scared."

I nod, my eyes blurry with tears. I *am* scared. Scared that Mom won't get better, and scared of what will happen to me if she doesn't. I tell this to Olympia.

Olympia's face softens. "You can't predict the future, Kat, but you've got your family to help you through this. And you've got me. Don't forget that." She smiles and gets up from the floor. "You're stronger than you think."

Her words hit me like a stun gun. I've never thought of myself as strong before. I picture myself as a strong-man in the circus, the old-fashioned kind, with thick, muscly legs and a twisty mustache, hoisting a pair of barbells high overhead. And it's that superhuman strength that gives me the courage to take the next jelly bean and ask the question that's been eating at me for weeks. I look Olympia straight in the eye. "Will I get OCD too?"

Olympia doesn't flinch or even look surprised. "I wish I had a clear-cut answer for you, Kat, but I don't. OCD has a genetic component, which means it tends to run in families. But that doesn't mean you'll get it. It's just a possibility."

This is not what I wanted to hear. It's not bad news exactly, but it isn't good news either. Olympia must sense my worry, because she adds: "It couldn't hurt to keep an eye on things, though—and to check in with a therapist, if you feel like it."

"My dad wants me to do that. My mom too."

"That's good," Olympia says. "Is that something you want to do?"

I shrug. For now, sharing jelly beans with Olympia feels like enough.

As I'm getting up to leave, Olympia goes over to the bookshelf and takes out a thick hardcover. She places it in my hands. "It's for you," she says. "I think it may help."

When I look at the title, I can understand why. The book is called *When Parents Aren't Perfect: Loving a Family Member with Anxiety and Other Mental Health Issues*. Then I read the name of the author: Olympia Rabinowitz, PhD. I look up, surprised. "You wrote this?"

Olympia smiles. "I did."

"That's so cool." I clutch the book to my chest. I know I should say more, but I'm speechless. Olympia wrote a book. For kids like me.

"I think you're ready for this," Olympia tells me.

"I am," I say. And at that moment, I know it's true.

30.

Trick or Treat

I'm leaving Olympia's office when I spot Hermione Granger—aka Halle—at her locker, putting her books away. Dumbledore is next to her, fiddling with his beard.

"Why aren't you wearing a costume?" Dumbledore/Michael says when he sees me. "It's Halloween!" If he knew about *Clean Sweep*, he wouldn't ask. And Halle? She wouldn't ask even if she *did* know. I still can't believe she's not talking to me.

"I like your Hermione costume," I tell Halle. "You look cute."

Halle slams her locker. "Did I say you could talk to me?"

"No, but since when do I need permission?"

"Since you don't care about being a good friend *and* you tried to steal my boyfriend, you sneaky—"

"Ladies, please!" Michael steps in between us.

Halle bops him on the head with her wizard wand and runs over to Thing 1 and Thing 2 (Coco and Madeline) who are giggling with Wonder Woman (Liberty) across the hall.

I feel my shoulders sag. I've never experienced this kind of rejection before—the achy kind that settles in your bones. But now, watching Halle laughing with her friends, I know what it feels like.

"You look sad," Michael says, patting my arm.

"I am sad," I say.

"I'm sad you're sad."

I'm not sure what to say next. Saying, "Thank you for caring" would be weird, and "I'm sad you're sad I'm sad" would be weirder. Luckily, I don't have to say anything. Halle is back. "Why are you talking to Michael?" she demands.

"I'm not," I say. "He was talking to me."

"Well, I don't like it."

I shrug. "It's not my fault."

"*Everything*," Halle says, "is your fault."

"What if it's not?" I say. "What if this has been a huge misunderstanding, like Olympia said, and it's *nobody's* fault?"

"I don't think that's possible," Michael says, adjusting his pointy cap. "Nothing can be nobody's fault. Unless the nobody is a somebody, which would mean it's actually somebody's fault."

Halle whacks him again with her wand.

"*Ow!*" Michael's hands fly to his head. "That hurt."

"Don't be such a baby," Halle says. She grabs his arm and steers him away from me. "Let's go."

✌

I make it through the rest of the day, hanging with Sam and avoiding Halle until it's dismissal. Dad is waiting for me outside the school building. "Why aren't you at work?" I ask, zipping up my jacket. "Is something wrong with Barbara? Is Henry okay?"

"Everybody's fine," Dad says, taking my backpack. "I just thought we'd have an early dinner first."

"First?"

"Uh, before you pass out Halloween candy."

"Oh." Then I notice the shopping bag in Dad's hand. When I try to peek inside, he pulls it away from me. "Why can't I look?" I ask.

"Because you can't." Dad waggles his eyebrows at me. He takes my hand and leads me to the Starlight Diner.

After we've had cheeseburgers followed by cake for dessert, Dad says he has a surprise for me. He reaches into his jacket pocket and pulls out a blindfold.

Huh?

"What's that for?" I ask.

"No questions," Dad says, tying the blindfold around

my eyes. "You'll find out soon enough." He takes my arm and leads me down the block.

"Where are we going?" I say, ignoring Dad's no-questions rule. "Uptown? Downtown? East? West?" Either way, I hope it's not far. Walking around blind-folded is not my idea of a good time, plus there's dog poop to consider and a Snapple cap I could miss.

"I said no questions," Dad repeats. "And no peeking either. That would be cheating."

"I wasn't going to," I say. And I wasn't. But now as we're rounding the corner, the suspense is killing me.

Finally we stop walking. "Ready?" Dad asks, leaning over to untie my blindfold.

"Ready," I say.

When Dad takes off the blindfold, I suck in my breath. We're standing in front of Halle's building. "What are we doing here?" I ask.

Dad grins like a jack-o'-lantern. "If the mountain won't come to Muhammad, then Muhammad must go to the mountain."

I must be Muhammad.

"Um, this is really nice of you, Dad, but I think we should go home. I don't want to miss the trick-or-treaters."

Dad's eyebrows spring up in surprise. "I thought you'd be happy to spend Halloween with your best friend."

Halle *was* my best friend, I want to tell him, before

she decided I was a backstabbing crush stealer. But how can I say that? It would ruin Dad's surprise. I let him take me into Halle's building and up in the elevator.

Mrs. Maklansky greets us at the door in bunny ears. She's also holding a carrot. "What a wonderful idea to get the girls together," she says, winking at Dad. "I'm so glad you suggested it, Dennis."

What's with the wink, I wonder? Does Mrs. Maklansky know Halle and I are fighting? Or does she know about Mom? And if she does, did she tell Halle? But that's impossible. Halle would have said something to me in school, even if she's still mad. I know she would. Well, I *think* she would.

Halle's mom straightens her bunny ears and calls out to her daughter. "Hal! Look who's here!"

When Halle joins us in the entrance hall in her Hermione costume, she looks ready to throw her mom to the werewolves. I can't say I blame her. I'm ready to do the same with Dad.

"I got you a costume, Kit-Kat," Dad says, handing me the shopping bag. "Take a look." I dip my hand inside and pull out a tall red-and-white-striped hat. "The Kat in the Hat," Dad explains. "Get it?"

I get it, all right. I just don't want it.

"Put it on," Dad says. "I want to see how it looks on you."

I give Dad the stink eye, but he doesn't pick up on it. I put on the hat.

"Adorable!" Mrs. Maklansky says, gesturing with her carrot. "Such a clever idea."

"It was a last-minute thing," Dad says, looking pleased. "I think it works."

"Oh, it *does*." Mrs. Maklansky's bunny ears bobble in agreement.

Halle just snorts.

"Well, I'd better leave you kids to it," Dad says, rubbing his hands together. "Have fun!"

I won't, and neither will Halle, but we fake-smile good-bye as Mrs. Maklansky brings Dad to the door.

Once the grown-ups are gone, I wait for Halle to say something about Mom—but she doesn't. This means either (a) she doesn't know or (b) she doesn't care. If it's (a), I could always tell her, but then she'd be nice to me out of pity. Instead, I take the pillowcase she's handing me and follow her out the door.

Although we're barely talking, we agree to start on the top floor, the twentieth, and work our way down, stopping at the apartments with paper pumpkins on the doors. That's the building's code for These Nice People Will Give You Candy. No paper pumpkin = Try Another Apartment.

We run to the first pumpkin we see, apartment 20H, and push the buzzer. A tiny white-haired lady opens the door. "My, my, my," she says, reaching for her glasses. "What have we here? The Cat in the Hat and . . ." She squints at Halle. "I don't know what you are, dear."

"Hermione Granger," Halle tells her. "From the Harry Potter books. Trick or treat!"

The old lady smiles and drops a king-size Snickers bar into Halle's pillowcase, then one into mine.

"Thank you," we say.

We race down to the nineteenth floor and score Skittles, Twizzlers, and peppermint patties from 19A and 19G. The other apartments don't bother to open up, even though they have paper pumpkins on their doors.

The same happens on seventeen, sixteen, and fifteen—Halle's floor. "What's wrong with these people?" Halle wants to know. "Don't they know Halloween is, like, a national holiday?"

It's not, but there's no way I'm pointing that out.

We run downstairs to the twelfth floor (there's no thirteen, bad luck), but it's as disappointing as the upper floors. Eleven isn't much better. "I don't get it," Halle says. "My neighbors are heartless."

Thankfully, the tenth, ninth, eighth, and seventh floors have more to offer. By the time we reach six, our pillowcases are bulging with candy. "This is more like it," Halle says, nodding. She marches over to 6B and presses the buzzer. We stand back and wait. "Someone better be home," she grumbles. "Or else."

A skinny lady in a hot-pink jogging suit opens the door. "Pardon my appearance," she says, gathering her hair into a messy bun. "I've been doing facial yoga."

Halle and I trade nervous glances.

"I know it sounds odd," the lady says, "but exercising the muscles in your face is very important. If I didn't do it, I'd probably need a face-lift."

"Um, trick or treat?" Halle holds out her pillowcase.

The lady continues. "There's this exercise I do . . . the lion? You inhale for a count of eight, then look up to the ceiling and stick out your tongue. Like this." Before we can stop her, the lady in 6B is demonstrating the lion with a deep, breathy *huhhhhhhhhhh*, her tongue darting out like a lizard's. "You girls should try it," she says, "before the first signs of aging start to appear."

"That's okay," Halle says, turning to go.

"Wait!" The lady disappears and comes back with two overripe bananas. "One for each of you." She drops the spotty fruit into our pillowcases. "Happy Halloween!"

Halle and I cover our mouths to keep from laughing. Then we run.

31.

Two Left Sneakers

"That lady was something else," I say, following Halle into her apartment. "Who gives out old bananas?"

Halle whips around to face me. "We're not doing this, Kat."

"Doing what?"

"Pretending we're friends."

"But I thought—"

"You thought wrong. Now, if you'll get out of my way, I have candy to count." Halle pushes past me and runs off to her room.

Alone by the front door with my pillowcase of candy, I take off my striped hat and slide down against the wall. I'm dying to send Dad a come-and-get-me text, but he won't be back to pick me up for another half hour. Changing plans would look fishy. Plus I can't give up now. As Ole Golly tells Harriet, life is a struggle, but a good spy gets in there and fights. I get up and walk down the hall to Halle's room.

"Open up, Hal," I say to the closed door. "Please."

"Go away!"

I jiggle the knob, but the door is locked. "Come on, Halle. We need to talk. This is messed up."

Halle pokes her head out. "*Messed up?* You're messed up for thinking you can be my friend again! You wouldn't listen to me when I needed to talk about Michael, and you wouldn't ask him out for me either." Halle jabs an angry finger into my chest. "Do you think it was easy for me to get up the courage to talk to him, Kat? Do you?" She doesn't wait for me to answer. "It was *not*. But you didn't care. You were just thinking about yourself. Now go!" She storms back inside and slams the door.

"Halle!" I yell. "Let me explain."

But she refuses to open up. She just puts on her music and cranks it up loud.

While I'm figuring out what to do next, Mrs. Maklansky appears in her bathrobe. She's ditched the carrot but is still wearing her bunny ears. "What's going on?" she asks. "I heard yelling."

"Oh, that." I try to think of an excuse. "We were just talking over the music. I didn't realize we were so loud."

"Really?" Halle's mom doesn't look convinced.

"Well . . ."

Mrs. Maklansky knocks on Halle's door. I hold my breath, worried she'll ask Halle what's really going on. But she doesn't. She just wants to know whether she should order pizza.

"No!" Halle yells through the closed door. "Kat's not staying!"

Mrs. Maklansky turns to me, embarrassed. "I don't know what's gotten into her, honey. That was incredibly rude."

I think of *Harriet the Spy*, when Sport's dad asks Harriet to join them for a steak dinner and Sport shouts "No!" Harriet feels terrible, but she doesn't cry. I won't either. I tell Mrs. Maklansky I'll wait for my dad in the lobby, and head down the hall to get my things.

Mrs. Maklansky follows me. "Your dad isn't due for at least thirty minutes," she says. "I insist you wait here with me."

There's no arguing with Mrs. Maklansky. Like mother, like daughter. Once we've sat down in the living room, she takes off her bunny ears. "Your dad told me what's going on with your mom," she says. "I'm so sorry, Kat."

"Thanks," I say, wishing my dad would hurry up. "My mom will be fine."

"Of course she will." Mrs. Maklansky gives my shoulder a squeeze. "But you know we're here if you need anything, or if you want to stay over. You're welcome anytime."

"Thanks," I say again. "That's really nice of you."

Mrs. Maklansky waves away my comment. "I'm not just being nice, I mean it. That's what friends are for. And you and Halle *are* friends, by the way—no matter what's going on between the two of you. Remember that."

"I'll try," I say, hoping Halle will too.

❧

Later, after Dad brings me back to his place, I have trouble falling asleep. It's not from the wheezy snores coming from Henry's side of the room, or because the trundle bed is lumpier than a bowl of oatmeal. It's because of Halle. Sure, we've had arguments before— over silly stuff, like who gets the window seat on class trips or the last slice of pizza. But we've never said mean things to each other, or just not talked. I can't even tell her about Mom. It feels wrong, like wearing two left sneakers. I roll out of bed and find my phone.

Are you there?

I give Halle a few minutes to answer my text.

I try again.

I don't want to fight

I sit back and wait.

Nothing.

She must still be counting her candy or reading *Harriet the Spy*. I'll give her a few more minutes.

Halle?

Nothing.

HALLE!

Still nothing.

I plug my charger into my phone and go back to bed. When I lie down, I feel like an elephant is sitting on my chest. I switch positions, but the pain is still there. *Thanks a lot, Halle.* I'll never get to sleep now.

I sit up in bed and dig around for something to read. The book Olympia gave me is within grabbing distance, so I pick it up and turn to the first chapter, "Understanding OCD." I dig out my flashlight and start reading. I don't remember falling asleep, but when I wake up the next morning, my flashlight is still on.

32.

Funny Little Hole

The elephant is still sitting on my chest three days later. Halle is still not talking to me, and I feel even lonelier without Mom. I decide to call her after school. "I miss you so much," I say, trying to keep my voice from wobbling.

"I miss you too, Kit-Kat," Mom says. "So much. The apartment feels empty without you."

"Then let me come home," I say. "Please."

Mom sighs. "I wish I could, honey. But I need to focus on my therapy. On getting better."

"Why can't you get better if I'm home with you?" I ask. "It's not fair."

"No, it isn't," she agrees. "But OCD isn't fair."

I have to think about that one. "What do you mean?" I finally ask.

Mom pauses before answering. "Well, it's something I have to deal with all the time, and I wish I didn't have to. Life would be so much easier without it."

Mom's right. Worrying about germs and keeping the house spotless and washing her hands all the time must feel horrible. It said so in Olympia's book. I guess life isn't fair for Mom either.

"But how are you, Kit-Kat?" Mom asks. "How's the Harriet project going? How's Halle?"

I hold back the tears. She's asking the right questions, but I don't want to add to her worries by answering them. "Good, Mom," I say. "Everything's good." This is not true, but small lies that make people feel better are not all bad. Maybe my fib will make Mom feel better too.

I'm still thinking about my conversation with Mom after we hang up, and, later, while I'm doing my homework. Talking to her was nice, but the elephant-on-my-chest feeling won't go away. The two most important people in my life, Mom and Halle, have disappeared, practically overnight, and all that's left is a huge, empty hole. I feel my eyes brimming with tears.

As I reach for a tissue, I remember that Harriet felt the exact same way. She wrote about it in her notebook. I grab *Harriet the Spy* out of my backpack and find the page I'm looking for. I start reading: "There's a funny little hole in me that wasn't there before, like a splinter in your finger, but this is somewhere above my stomach."

I have the same hole. The question is, what can I do to make it go away?

And then I have an idea.

I get my laptop and open my email. But it's not Olympia I'm writing to this time.

TO: Halle.Maklansky@VillageHumanity.org
SUBJECT: Forgive me
DATE: November 3 4:43:02 PM EDT
FROM: Kat.Greene@VillageHumanity.org

Dear Halle,

    I know you're mad and don't want to hear anything I have to say. But I'm going to say it anyway. I never tried to steal Michael away from you. I'm your best friend and would never do something like that. I could've been a better friend, though. As you said, working up the courage to talk to Michael wasn't easy. I should've listened and helped you somehow. I miss you so much, Hal. I hope you'll write back.

Love,

Kat xoxoxoxox

I reread my email, deciding whether or not to say something about Mom. I leave it alone. If Halle writes back, I want her to do it because she misses me and accepts my apology, not because my mom has OCD and she feels sorry for me.

I take a deep breath and press Send, imagining my email soaring through cyberspace and landing in Halle's inbox with a soft, satisfying *plink*.

33

Field Trip

The "funny little hole" in me continues to grow, until a week's gone by and Halle still hasn't answered my email. She's also not talking to me when Jane tells us to choose bus partners for the field trip to the Tate Seashell Museum, in lower Manhattan. We're leaving in ten minutes.

"I still don't see why we have to go to a seashell museum," Michael says, getting up from his seat. "Can't we go somewhere fun? Like Laser Quest? I think there's one in Brooklyn."

"Now, there's a brilliant idea," Madeline says, putting down her magazine. "Laser tag in Brooklyn. Funsies."

I hold my breath, waiting for Halle to stick up for

her crush. To say that going all the way to Brooklyn to play laser tag is the best idea she's ever heard. She doesn't. She asks Sam to be her bus partner.

Huh? I knew Halle wouldn't pick me, but Sam? What happened to Michael?

I try to make sense of this weird new development while Jane herds us onto the school bus, and later, hurries us in line to get tickets at the museum. But I can't wrap my head around it. Instead, I focus on our tour guide, an old lady with hair the color of pigeon poop. Her name is Mrs. Stouffer, Jane tells us, and we're free to ask questions.

Kevin raises his hand. "Are you wearing a wig?" I look over at Halle to exchange eye rolls, until I remember she's ignoring me.

Jane blushes a deep red and gives Kevin a stare down. "You don't have to answer that, Mrs. Stouffer. In fact, I'd prefer you didn't."

"Very well, then." Mrs. Stouffer coughs into her hanky and continues. "Before we begin, children, you should know that the shells in this exhibit represent a tiny fraction of the offshore populations hidden under the sand or among the corals, sponges, and sea-fan meadows of our local bodies of water."

I feel my eyes glaze over. It's as if Mrs. Stouffer is trying to lull us to sleep. Or worse, hypnotize us into spending lots of money in the gift shop. Little does she know that the last time our class came face-to-face with consumer goods—last year, at the Museum of Natural History—Kevin got caught shoplifting a plastic dinosaur.

Sam, who's been taking notes, looks up from his legal pad. "I was wondering . . . How many shells are in the museum's collection?"

Mrs. Stouffer reaches for her glasses. "You're not asking for an exact figure—are you, dear?"

Sam nods.

"Oh, my." Our tour guide titters nervously. "I don't really know. The curators have counted them, of course, but—"

"Just ballpark it," Sam says. "I'm really curious."

Out of habit I try to catch Halle's eye, but she's staring at Sam as if he's asked the most fascinating question ever. I wonder if she's feeling all right.

Meanwhile, Mrs. Stouffer has shuffled over to a giant *Wheel of Fortune*–like contraption—the Shell Classification Wheel, she tells us—and asks Kevin to give it a spin. "I'd like to buy a vowel!" he yells.

I want to laugh, but the *Clean Sweep* disaster is still fresh in my mind.

After identifying an apple murex, which looks nothing like an apple, and a horse conch, which looks nothing like a horse, Mrs. Stouffer stops spinning and suggests we have a look at the museum's exciting array of scallops.

"I'm allergic to scallops," Hector announces.

"Me too," Kevin says. "I get a rash all over, and I itch really bad."

"Bad*ly*," Jane corrects him.

"I have eczema," Sam adds.

"An oatmeal bath is good for itchy skin," Liberty tells him, adjusting her nose stud. "Or a poultice made from dandelion, yellow dock root, and chaparral."

"I've already prescribed a steroid cream," Wilson says, pointing to Sam's arm. "Let's not complicate things."

"Steroids are filled with chemicals," Liberty sniffs. "Sam shouldn't have to—"

"If there are no more questions," Mrs. Stouffer says, "I think we should wrap it up."

"Excellent idea!" Jane steps forward to thank our guide for the wonderful tour and asks us to follow her outside. When I turn around, Mrs. Stouffer is massaging her temples with her fingertips.

On the bus I sit toward the back with Coco. Sam and Halle are in the row in front of us. Their heads are so close together, they look like the Two-Headed Monster from *Sesame Street*. "That's silly," Halle says, giggling. "How could a Chihuahua lift a horse? There's no way!"

Sam says something I can't make out, and Halle erupts in a fresh fit of giggles.

Coco gives me a poke. "Looks like someone's got a new boyfriend."

"You don't know what you're talking about," I say. "She's just being nice." I'm still mad at Halle for ignoring me, but I can't have Coco making things up about my ex-best friend.

"Looks like more than 'just being nice' to me," Coco says with a smirk. "I think it's *luuuuuv*."

Before I can tell her off, the bus is rounding Seventh Avenue and pulling up in front of school. I grab my backpack, zip up my jacket, and head down the aisle. Halle is standing right in front of me. She's so close I can smell her green-apple shampoo. I tap her on the shoulder.

Halle turns around and scowls. "What do you want?"

"Nothing much. Just wanted to say hi." I offer her a cheery smile, hoping she'll return it.

She doesn't—but she doesn't say anything mean either. I take this as a good sign.

34.

Another Chance

When I visit Mom for the first time over the weekend, she's wearing jeans and a Mickey Mouse sweatshirt—and there's no red bandanna in sight. It's been almost two weeks since I've seen her, and I wasn't sure what to expect. "Your head is naked," I say, pointing to her blond curls.

Mom touches her hair awkwardly. "It's part of my therapy. Not my idea, but if it helps . . ."

We're in my room, sorting through last year's summer clothes to give to Goodwill. Most of my stuff still fits, but a few of the T-shirts look like they belong on an American Girl doll. Some of the shorts too. Mom takes a too-small T-shirt from a pile on my bed and places it in the giveaway bag. "Aren't you proud of me, Kit-Kat?"

she says, gesturing to the bag at her feet. "I'm only toss-ing out the stuff *you* don't want."

Mom joking about her OCD = A very good thing.

Mom stops folding and sits down on the bed. She motions for me to join her. "I need to talk to you about something, honey."

I sit down next to her. "Okay . . ."

"I never apologized for frightening you the way I did," Mom says. "Or for hiding out in my room after I fainted. I should never have put you through that. It was wrong of me—and selfish."

I feel my throat catch. "It's not your fault, Mom. You couldn't help it."

"Maybe not," Mom says, offering me a sad smile. "But no parent wants to cause her child pain. And my OCD has done that to you—I know it." She reaches for my hand. "I don't expect you to understand this com-pletely, Kit-Kat, but I need you to try." She pauses before looking into my eyes. "I've always been an anx-ious person, ever since I can remember. I was able to deal with my anxiety pretty well for years—and even downplay it, to some extent. But it's finally caught up with me."

I nod, letting her know it's okay to go on.

"That's why I couldn't handle *Clean Sweep*, or the humiliation I felt afterward," Mom says. "I felt out of control and incredibly anxious. So I shut down."

I'm not sure what to say. I've never thought of my

mom as an anxious person, just overly cautious about things—like making me wear floaties in the pool after I'd already learned to swim, or triple-checking my hair for lice after outbreaks at school. It was Mom just being Mom. But now that she's admitting she's always been anxious, her behavior kind of makes sense. "I think I get what you're saying," I tell her. "But isn't it normal to worry about stuff that's bothering you?" Like how I worry about Halle being my friend again—or how she couldn't stop worrying about her crush.

Mom gives my hand a squeeze. "You're right, Kit-Kat. Everybody feels nervous sometimes. But OCD goes beyond that. It's an anxiety disorder, and the rituals you see me doing—cleaning obsessively, washing my hands—help me feel in control. I can't explain it fully, but I know it's not healthy. I'm learning new coping skills in therapy, though. Talking in Group helps too."

Group, Mom explains, is basically a rap session without the talking stick. It borders dangerously close to dirty-laundry territory if you ask me, but Mom must think it's helping her or she wouldn't do it. Still, I'm surprised she isn't embarrassed.

"Doesn't it feel weird to talk about your problems in front of a bunch of strangers?" I ask, remembering how hard it was for me to share in rap session the first time, and later, during my jelly-bean sessions with Olympia.

"It was at the beginning," Mom says. "But it's gotten easier. I actually enjoy it now."

I look at her in surprise. "You *enjoy* talking about your problems?"

Mom laughs. "Okay, *enjoy* is too strong a word. Talking about OCD is hard, and no one likes to admit they have a problem. But I think I'm up for the challenge."

I smile. I couldn't agree more.

Later that night Mom and I are playing Monopoly in the living room when the phone rings. "Ignore it," I say, moving my thimble three spaces. "I just got out of jail." But Mom can't let a ringing phone ring, so she jumps up to get it. Before I can ask who's calling, she's taken the phone into the kitchen.

My mind goes into overdrive as I wonder what happened. Maybe Mom's OCD is worse than I thought and she needs to go away for treatment. Maybe Dad is on the phone now, arranging to pick me up early so Mom can pack. But that's not likely. Mom ditched her bandanna, and she's talking in Group. That's got to count for something.

While I'm trying to figure out why Mom would take the phone into the other room, she comes back and takes her place at the Monopoly board. She doesn't look upset, though. She's grinning.

"Who was it?" I ask.

"You won't believe it." Mom's smile gets bigger.

"Tell me!"

Mom crisscrosses her legs. "Bing Monroe."

Huh? "Why would he be calling you?" I ask.

Mom picks up the dice and starts fiddling with them. "He said he feels bad about what happened on the show and asked whether I'd like to return for another chance at the big money."

Oh *no*. If Mom goes on *Clean Sweep* again, after everything she's been through—after everything *I've* been through—I don't think I could take it. "What did you tell him?" I brace myself for bad news.

Mom hands me the dice. "I thanked him for his offer but said I don't have time."

Relief hits me like a tsunami, until I realize Mom isn't telling the truth. She has plenty of time. She doesn't have a job, and I know she's not cleaning or washing her hands as much. I can see it with my own eyes. Plus we're playing Monopoly, which can take *hours*. The last time I played with Halle, we had to take snack breaks! I ask Mom to explain.

She holds up her hands and wiggles her fingers. "What do you see?" she asks.

I lean over for a closer look. "Your hands aren't as chapped," I say. "Or as red."

"Exactly. Which means . . ."

"You're not washing them as much."

"And . . . ?"

"Your therapy is working?"

Mom nods. "What else?"

"I'm not sure," I admit.

"Therapy takes up a lot of my time," Mom says. "Five days a week, plus every other weekend."

"Which means you're too busy to go on *Clean Sweep*," I say, finally getting it.

"Bingo," Mom says. "There's a group for family members too, if you're interested."

I think about my jelly-bean sessions with Olympia, and about her book. "That's okay," I say, handing Mom the dice. "It's your turn now."

Mom looks at me and smiles. She knows I'm not talking about Monopoly.

35.

What Would Harriet Do?

On the Monday before the Thanksgiving assembly, Olympia is standing next to Jane as she bangs the gong for attention. "I've noticed some tension in the room," Jane says, "and I think we should talk about it. Olympia has kindly agreed to join us for an emergency rap session."

"Emergency?" Wilson leaps out of his seat. "I've got a defibrillator in my locker."

"No one is sick, Wilson," Olympia says, gesturing for him to sit down. "This is an emergency of an emotional nature."

"Oh." Wilson flops back in his seat. I almost feel sorry for him. Unlike Madeline and Coco, who haven't stopped gossiping for weeks, Wilson doesn't know that

Jane is talking about me and Halle. But I don't want to talk about Halle. After all the jelly-bean sessions with Olympia, I'm all talked out. Besides, Halle won't talk to me.

Then again, I can't sit around and do nothing. But what can I do? Or, better yet: What would *Harriet* do?

I shut my eyes and picture all the jams Harriet gets herself into—on her spy route, with her parents, with her classmates. *Especially* with her classmates. Harriet doesn't know what to do, but Ole Golly does. Ole Golly has the answers to everything!

I can't remember what Ole Golly says exactly, so I reach into my desk and pull out my copy of *Harriet the Spy*. There it is, in black and white:

1) You have to apologize.
2) You have to lie.
Otherwise you are going to lose a friend.

I can do that, I tell myself. I'm not wild about the lying part, because look where that got me when I lied to Dad. But I can certainly apologize to Halle. Maybe I'm-sorry emails aren't enough.

Once Olympia has arranged our chairs in a circle, I put out my hand for the talking stick. When she gives it to me, her smile says it all: "Go, Kat!"

Clutching the stick, I look over at Halle. She's staring at her sneakers, but I know she's listening. "Halle,

I'm sorry for not being a better friend," I tell her, "and for not listening when you needed me to. I shouldn't have kept things from you either, Hal—things about me, and things that had to do with your crush. It was wrong of me, and I'm sorry."

Halle sits there stony-faced, her chin resting on her chest. When she looks up, her eyes are shiny with tears. "I should be the one apologizing to you, Kat," she says, reaching for the talking stick. "I mean, crushing on Michael? What was I thinking?"

Michael, who's been cleaning under his nails with a paper clip, is now on his feet. "What's *that* supposed to mean?"

Halle lowers her voice. "Sam told me how upset you were, Kat, but I didn't believe him. I thought he was just saying that to get us back together."

"Yeah, but—"

"And I overheard you talking to Coco on the bus, on the way back from the field trip. You stuck up for me, but I ignored you." Halle wipes her nose on the back of her sleeve. "I'm a horrible person."

"No, you're not," I say. "I wasn't a good friend. Friends don't have to like—or want to talk about—the same things. I should've known that."

Halle's eyes find mine. "After you left on Halloween, my mom told me about your mom. She wanted me to call you, but I wouldn't."

"It's no big deal," I say. "You were mad. I get it."

Halle hangs her head. "Still. I should've been there for you."

"Maybe, but—" Before I can say more, Halle jumps out of her seat and bolts out of the room.

"Halle?" Olympia calls after her. "Halle!"

It's too late. My best friend is gone.

My heart feels like a raisin, all dried up and shriveled. How did this happen? I apologized, just like Ole Golly tells Harriet to. But unlike Harriet, I didn't lie. Did I do something wrong?

Suddenly I hear the *squelch-squelch* of sneakers on the linoleum outside the classroom. Halle runs back in, holding a lumpy plastic bag. "Here," she says, thrusting the bag at me. I don't need to open it to know what's inside. Halle breaks into a wide grin. "Camels have three eyelids," she says.

"Oh, yeah?" I say, grinning back. "Slugs have four noses."

"Interesting," Halle says. "A snail breathes through its foot."

"And the Mona Lisa has no eyebrows," I add.

Halle stops smiling. "What's that got to do with a snail breathing through its foot?"

"Nothing," I say. "It's just another interesting Snapple fact."

Halle steps closer. "I've missed you, Kat."

"I missed you too, Hal."

Before you can say, "Pass the talking stick," Halle and

I rush at each other like long-lost relatives and hug each other tight. We stay that way for a long time, even though some of the boys are laughing at us. But who cares? I have my best friend back, and that's all that matters.

36.

That's What Counts

The Thanksgiving assembly is today and Mom won't be going. She told me last night on the phone. "I'm sorry, Kit-Kat," she said. "I thought I could do it, but I'm not ready. I hope you understand."

I do understand. I'm just disappointed.

Now, as I'm peering through the dusty red curtain, waiting for my moment to wow the crowd as The Boy with the Purple Socks, I feel a tap on my shoulder. It's Sam, as Pinky Whitehead, carrying an empty glass.

"For milk," he explains.

"Nice touch," I say, hoping the audience will get the reference. As Harriet says: "Pinky was so pale, thin, and weak that he looked like a glass of milk."

"I like what you've done too," Sam says, pointing to the sign I'm wearing:

ASK TO BE TOLD
THE LEGEND OF THE PURPLE SOCKS
10 CENTS

"And look." I show Sam my feet. "Green socks."

"Sweet!" Sam says.

I'm glad I remembered this detail. By the end of the book, the purple socks are up a flagpole.

As Sam runs off for milk, I watch as my classmates gather in the wings. Wilson has ditched his lab coat and is dressed as Sport, in a baseball cap and rumpled clothes; Coco, as Janie, has made pigtails and dotted her face with fake freckles. Madeline and Kevin, in matching plaid dresses as Marion Hawthorne and Rachel Hennessey, are off to the side arguing over who gets to go on first. Kevin is wearing his Burger King crown as usual, so I'm guessing they'll argue over that too.

Hector—aka *Mrs.* Welsch—surprises everyone by wearing a sequined cocktail dress and a long string of pearls. "My husband is holding my mink stole," he says, grinning at Liberty, who is wearing an altered tuxedo as Mr. Welsch.

Liberty holds up the stole. "It's not real fur," she says. "In case you were wondering."

"You look great, guys," I tell them. "Very authentic."

"Yeah, but look at me!" It's Michael, dressed as Ole Golly, in a tweed jacket and matching skirt. Halle, who's standing next to him as Harriet, looks even better. She's wearing an old pair of jeans, a dark-blue sweatshirt, blue sneakers with holes over each pinky toe, and black-rimmed glasses without lenses. To top it off, she's carrying a black-and-white composition notebook.

"Jane took away my Boy Scout knife," Halle says, patting her tool belt. "But I have everything else." I inspect her spy gear and see that she's right. There's a flashlight, a leather pouch for Harriet's notebook, a case for extra pens, and a water canteen.

At that moment, Jane appears with her clipboard. "Two minutes, Purple Socks. You too, Pinky Whitehead. Janie and Sport . . ." She cranes her neck for Coco and Wilson. "Stand by!"

I start to panic. "Where's Sam?" I scope the room for my partner. "Sam!"

"Right here," Sam says, reappearing with his milk. "You look scared."

"I am," I admit.

"We've gone over this a thousand times, Kat. You'll be fine. Stop worrying!"

Sam probably thinks I'm worried about messing up my lines, but he's wrong. I'm worried I might cry. I understand why Mom can't be here, but the thought of looking into the audience and not seeing her in it makes me sad. "I'm okay," I say, yanking up a droopy green sock. "Just a little nervous."

"Don't be. You'll be great." Sam gives me a little push in the direction of the stage. "It's now or never."

I'd prefer never, but I give Sam a wobbly smile, take a deep breath, and walk out past the red curtain.

"Kitty-Kat!" It's Henry, yelling from the front row. He climbs off Barbara's lap and windmills his arms. "Over HERE! With Mommy and Daddy! *Look!*"

My cheeks start to burn. Why couldn't Dad have dropped Henry off at preschool or left him with a babysitter? It would've saved everyone a lot of embarrassment, especially me. I'm so flustered I've forgotten my lines.

Sam runs onstage to save me. "This is The Boy with the Purple Socks," he says, pointing to the sign hanging around my neck. "His real name is Peter Matthews. He's new to school and has a story to tell. Don't you, Peter?" Sam gives me a gentle nudge. "*Go,*" he says under his breath.

As I'm about to open my mouth, I hear whispers in the front row, followed by loud shushing. Oh *no*. What is Henry up to now?

But it's not Henry who's making all the fuss.

It's Mom.

In shock, I watch as she climbs over Barbara's legs and takes a seat next to Dad. When she catches my eye, she waves.

I know I'm supposed to start speaking. To tell the audience why I wear purple—and now green—socks. But how can I focus on socks? Mom is here when she said she wouldn't be. It's a miracle. Still, the show must go on. "My name is Peter Matthews," I say, "but everyone calls me The Boy with the Purple Socks. I'm wearing green ones now"—I lift up my pants leg to show off my socks—"but this is a big change for me."

And that's when I realize that The Boy with the Purple Socks isn't the only one who's changed. I look to my family beaming up at me from their front-row seats, and my heart feels ready to burst. I manage to keep it together until Sam takes over as Pinky Whitehead, but my hands are still shaking when I run offstage. I can't believe I got through it. And Mom was there. Wow, and more wow.

"You were great!" Sam says, giving me a high five.

"No, *you* were," I say. "You totally saved me!"

"I've always got your back, Kat," Sam says. "You know that."

I do.

After the entire class takes a bow together, Jane invites the guests to the classroom for punch and cookies. It's a hectic scene, with parents congratulating one another and kids running around in their costumes. Kevin has ditched his Rachel Hennessey dress but is still wearing the Burger King crown. Some things never change.

I spot Dad right away, helping himself to chocolate-chip cookies. He grins when he sees me. "Brava!" he says, handing me a cookie. "Or, should I say, bravo?"

I giggle. "Where's Mom? Did she leave with Barbara and Henry?" I wouldn't be surprised if she did. As she told me over the phone last night, she's still adjusting to her thoughts about wanting to clean things and avoiding germs.

Dad says, "I'm afraid so, honey. You know . . ."

I feel my heart sink. I don't blame Mom for leaving, but it would've been nice if she'd stayed to congratulate me. Oh well. I swipe another cookie off Dad's plate and dive back into the crowd.

I'm fighting my way to the punch bowl when I feel a tap on my shoulder. My heart beats fast as I turn around. I knew Mom wouldn't let me down!

But it's not Mom I see. It's Olympia.

"You were wonderful, Kat," she says, leaning in for a hug. "Congratulations!"

I try to hide my disappointment, but Olympia sees right through me. "Your mom isn't here, is she?"

"No," I say, feeling my shoulders sag. "She was for a little while, but she had to leave."

"Yes, but she *was* here," Olympia reminds me. "And that's what counts." She gives me a wink. "Remember that."

"I will," I say, deciding she's right. "Thanks."

Olympia smiles. "Now, if you'll excuse me, there's a cookie with my name on it. Enjoy the party!"

While I'm watching Olympia head for the food table, Kevin appears and plops the Burger King crown on my head. "Nice job, Sock Boy!"

"She was good, wasn't she?" It's Sam, a milk mustache above his upper lip.

"You weren't so bad yourself," I tell Sam. I'm about to ask how he remembered all his lines when Halle races up to us, the tools on her spy belt jangling.

"We did it, Kat! We survived!"

I laugh, knowing what she means by "survived." Michael acted silly and flubbed most of his lines. If it weren't for Halle, their presentation would've been a disaster.

"I like what you did with The Boy with the Purple Socks," Halle tells me. "It was a real crowd pleaser."

"Yeah," I say, "but I messed up at the beginning. If it weren't for Sam, I don't know what I would've done." I look over at Sam to trade grins. We both know he came to the rescue, in more ways than one.

Sam turns to Halle. "You were great as Harriet," he says. "Everybody said so."

"That's right," I agree. "You were a rock star, Hal. No one could've done it better."

Halle looks at me in surprise. "You mean it?"

"I do," I say, smiling wide. "I honestly do."

37

A Little Lighter

A huge bouquet of flowers is waiting for me on the kitchen counter when Dad and I get back to his place. "They're beautiful," I say to Barbara. "Thank you!"

Barbara smiles. "I'd love to take the credit, but they're not from me."

"They're not?"

"Nope." She points to a small white envelope next to the flower vase. "Take a look at the card."

I tear open the envelope and start reading:

Congratulations to my favorite Purple
(and Green) Sock Boy. You rocked it, Kit-Kat!
All my love,
Mom xoxo

The goofiest grin spreads across my face. Mom didn't stay for the party, but this is the next best thing. I can't wait to thank her when I see her at Thanksgiving. But first, I want to tell Halle about my beautiful flowers.

"Can I make a call from your office?" I ask Dad after Barbara tells me that Henry is napping in our shared room. "I have something to tell Halle."

"Oh, of *course*," Dad says with an exaggerated head slap. "It's only been thirty minutes since you girls last spoke."

"Very funny, Dad."

I head for Dad's office to call Halle, but first go over to the window in the living room and take a look outside. The city looks different from Dad's apartment. It's quieter in Yorkville, with fewer cabs and bikes. There are fewer people on the sidewalk, walking dogs and pushing strollers. I don't hear jackhammers or yelling. It all makes me feel a little lighter. Happy, even. Not happier than living at Mom's, of course. I can't wait until she's ready for me to come home. But living at Dad's hasn't been horrible either. Just different.

And maybe, just maybe, different is not so bad.

Acknowledgments

Ever since I could hold a Dixon Ticonderoga No. 2 pencil, it's been my dream to write a book. And when that dream becomes a reality? There are no words. Okay, that's not true. There are words. Thankful words. I'd like to share them here.

Gratitude beyond measure to Kathleen Rushall, who championed *Kat* from the beginning and sealed the deal, and to my amazing agent, Patricia Nelson, whose unflagging support carried me to the finish line.

To my fabulous editor, Julie Bliven, whose immense talent and keen editorial eye is evident on every page. Not only did you make *Kat* shine like the top of the Chrysler Building (☺), you are one of the loveliest people I've ever met. My novel sparkles because of you, Julie. Thank you.

To the dedicated team at Charlesbridge, including eagle-eyed copyeditor Hannah Mahoney, who taught me that aka has no periods and jelly bean is two words (who knew?), and to publicity maven Donna Spurlock for her tireless promotion of *Kat*. To Nathan Durfee for his dazzling cover and chapter illustrations, and to art director Susan Sherman for commissioning him.

To Sara Lewis Murre, life coach extraordinaire, who helped me to achieve my dream of becoming a novelist. There would have been no Kat if it weren't for you, Sara. My gratitude to you is infinite.

To Nancy Butts, who entered my life as an editor and stayed as a friend. Nancy, you are my Spinal Sister forever. Bone-crushing hugs to you!

To Lara Williamson, whose unstinting across-the-pond support kept me going, draft after draft after draft. You lifted me up and cheered me on with your wisdom, warmth, and wit. I am lucky to call you my Peaboddy Pal.

To Dr. Alexandra Barzvi and Dr. Silvia W. Olarte, who aided my research by providing clinical insight into OCD, and to memoirist Traci Foust, who shared her personal struggle with the disorder in a flurry of back-and-forth emails.

To my writing buddy, Rose Cirigliano, whose friendship, wine, and Nino's pizza nurtured and sustained me.

To David Wong, who read multiple drafts of the manuscript and provided invaluable insight. If bigwigging doesn't work out for you, David, you know who to call.

To my early *Kat* readers: Irene Hwang, Marni Mann, Meredith Summa, and Amy Nagler. Your comments helped make the novel stronger. *Mwah!*

To Denise and John Biondo, who built my beautiful website and advised me on all things techie. Thanks for all your hard work, guys!

The path to publication is bumpier than a cab hurtling down Fifth Avenue, but my writer friends have made the ride smoother. Thanks to Camille Di Maio, Eileen Palma, Steven Tate, Janice Nimura, and Stacy Schiff.

To my agent sisters—aka #TheRevisionists—who are the most enthusiastic cheerleaders I know. All together now: "How great is Patricia Nelson?!?"

A special shout out to the Giles Twins, Amy and Jeff, and to Stephanie Elliot, whose daily talk-me-down-from-the-ledge missives never failed to make me smile. To the #2017Debuts, for signal boosts, fist-bumps, and writerly camaraderie. Gratitude beyond measure to Jonathan Rosen, Sally J. Pla, Katy White, Peternelle van Arnsdale, Kristin L. Gray, Christina June, and Jilly Gagnon.

To the Nerdy Book Club for hosting my cover reveal.

Kat Greene Comes Clean is not autobiographical, but I wouldn't be coming clean if I neglected to mention that Kat's fictional school, the Village Humanity School, was inspired by my own alma mater, the venerable City and Country School, in New York's Greenwich Village. City and Country is responsible for teaching me to think outside the box.

To my C&C classmates: there are no friends like old friends. Daniel Alperin, Clifton English Kew, Noah

Evans, Will Smith, Paul Canosa, Nicole Batchelor Regne, Scott Fierman, Michael Oppizzi . . . I'm talking to YOU.

And to the real-life Halle, China Jorrin, whose friendship left an indelible imprint on my life. You will always be the Iggy to my Mouse. (Or is it the Mouse to my Iggy?)

To the outstanding educators at the Brearley School, with special thanks to librarians Amy Chow and Patricia Aakre for helping me to navigate the independent-school library scene, and to the Dwight School, for welcoming me with open arms.

To the memory of the late great Louise Fitzhugh, author of my beloved *Harriet the Spy*, which defined my childhood and inspired me to become a writer. Louise, you and I would have been great friends.

And speaking of friends, I've been blessed with the best. I would like to acknowledge some of my oldest and dearest here: Kerry Zaimes, Robert Lischinsky and Tony Frye, Costa and Simone Peridakis, Jonathan Wachtel, Sonia Stephens, Gbenro Adegbola, Lauren Sobel Prario, Emily Baller, Papüs Sissoko, Rebecca Meyer, Mike Nealy, Maura Parker Quinlan, Adrian Wilck, Diane Seo, Jennifer Schecter, Pam Selin, Margie Sung, Amy Muntner, Anita Naik, Daniel Lewis, Mitch Yesagare, Julie Mardin, Millie Eng-Martinez, and the Tropp-Levy family. Thank you for putting up with me over the years. It couldn't have been easy.

To my in-laws, Heinz and Inge Roske, and to my sister-in-law, Harriet Roske, whose familial loyalty and fierce support are appreciated enormously. Ditto to the Schultz, Karstadt, and Rosoff families. Thank you, guys!

To my parents, Les and Sheila Karstadt, who read my first novel, *Beyond the Lily Pond*—written at C&C when I was ten—and encouraged me to keep going. Thank you for indulging my wild imagination. That couldn't have been easy either.

To my exceptional daughter, Chloe Roske, whose close reading and astute editorial comments shaped the manuscript in more ways than I can verbalize. Bumby, you are my sun, my moon, my stars . . . my heart. I am lucky to be your mother.

To my wonderful husband, Henry Roske, who has been by my side for almost three decades and who continues to amaze me with his kindness, intelligence, and unconditional support. Henry, I couldn't have done this without you. *Quack quack.*